from HONEY *with love*

my Life *as a* Second-Chance Dog

ALLEN PAUL

ILLUSTRATED BY AMIRA KOTZE

Sky Pony Press
New York

Contents

PART ONE
Leaving Home

1
Deep in the Swamp

In the bald cypress swamp where I was born, the alligator was king. Papa always said the big 'uns were mean-snake sly and fly-snatchin' fast. Imagine one of those half-sunk rascals posin' as a harmless log. Some poor critter moseys by and quick as a flash it pops up and zaps 'em. That lowdown stunt was the worst we'd ever heard tell of in the swamp.

Every so often the gator fakin' got so bad our swamp elders posted travel alerts on the Critter Trail. The warnin' signs said to watch for bubblin' logs. To avoid those devils half sunk in the muck, us pups had to take the Beast Feast Detour.

Can't tell you how many times Mama would say, "Now girl, you keep a close watch out for gator logs." She worried I'd forget just once and get turned into a two- or three-bite meal. That scary thought caused many a nightmare of thirteen-foot gators. In the worst, I stepped on one with huge gapin' jaws and snarly rows of teeth. It took a vicious swipe at me that just missed, and I ran flat out through the marsh. No matter how I zigged and zagged, the gator kept gainin' and gainin'. Pretty soon it was snappin' at my tail with bone-crushin' chomps. I was a goner for sure when the ole soap bubble popped. As I came to, it felt like my tail got whacked and I told myself: *You can't be a dog without a tail—not even a mutt.* A quick check and . . . whew, it was still back there, but so was a chilly draft that kept blowin' just short of a gale. Bad dreams can mess with your head that way, especially when you've just turned one year old which is not much more'n a nursin' pup.

Afterward, Mama always nuzzled my nose and asked, "Same bad dream?" I'd turn belly up and get the licks that calmed my pantin' and shakin'. But that didn't make the dreams go away. In another dream a sly, grinnin' gator said, "Hop on my back and I'll ride you across the pond." I knew the story of the frog that did that and never made it across . . . so I took off lickety-split for the high ground. That two-faced gator gave chase and 'fore long it, too, was snappin' at my tail. Once again, the ole soap bubble popped, and I felt another backside draft. At the time, I just wanted Mama to make it go away. Later on, when she wasn't there, I came to understand what those little gales were sayin': The threat is always back there. 'Stead of Mama, I s'pose my wild genes were doin' the talkin'. If you're part of a vanishin' breed like me, you need wild genes to tell you when and what to dodge. Trust me: you can't survive in the swamp without 'em.

Like Mama, my wild genes also told me to keep a close eye on gators. I watch 'em now glidin' through the early mornin' fog like somebody polin' by in a skiff . . . feedin' on cottonmouths, crunchy turtles, or some poor possum dozin' on the bank. In the spring, ornery males crawl out of wallowin' holes lookin' for females to court. They'll roam a mile or so through the muck bellowin' all the way. When our pack hears that hullabaloo, we high-tail it up the ridge to the black gum thicket where our den is hid. 'Til the lovesick boys calm down, we only go out for quick hunts close by. Never seen a big 'un up on the ridge, but Mama still reminds me I could be a two- or three-bite meal.

But that weren't the worst of it. Sometimes she'd say, "If the gator misses, then the Phantom will get you for sure." Those words always sent a shiver down my spine. I didn't know much about the Phantom—only that it was a four-legged critter that showed itself in a lightnin' storm at Silver Bluff. When the lightnin' flashed, there it stood, high on the cliff above the big river which was slam full of gators.

Sound scary? Lemme just say the swamp's got a soft side too—it ain't all mean by any stretch. The early mornin' fog creeps in like smoke from a slow-burnin' peat fire. A light breeze stirs and unfurls fluffy beards of Spanish moss, and the limbs reach through the dewy haze like giant bird talons. When the fog lifts its skirts even more, you can see the swamp's greatest wonder: giant cypress domes all flattened out on top, which is why we call 'em bald. Papa says the domes are the swamp's umbrella that shades the critters when the sun beats down. By mid-mornin' when the ground clouds clear, it gets so hot the critters just snooze or watch the butterfly army marchin' to the purple milkweed patch. The tawny-orange monarchs can snack there to their heart's content. Like I said, the swamp's got a soft side too.

Even so, our elders always say, "The Critter Trail ain't easy street. No one gets off scratch free." Papa says the proper term is "Scot free," and what they mean is sooner or later you're bound to get bit and maybe bit hard.

When I finally got whacked, I thought the soap bubble would soon pop, that Mama would then nuzzle my nose and say everything was okay. But that didn't happen, and I soon knew no dream was messin' with my head. You might say the mornin' fog finally had lifted its skirts, and I had no place to dodge or hide. I was part of a vanishin' breed—just like the dodo bird. All I could do was wish with my eyes closed and my paw nails crossed that my wild genes would kick in and somehow save me.

2

Jaws of Steel

Never shoulda chased that sorry skunk through the mornin' fog, or any time for that matter. Sooner or later the little yuckster was bound to foul up somethin', and even if he didn't squirt his yucky perfume, and even if I did catch him, I wouldn't wish skunk meat on a lurkin' log. It's worse'n roadkill . . . okay, trail kill if you'd druther.

I'd let down my guard. Sometimes, with no warnin' at all, I'd forget to listen to the wild genes that alert me to danger. When that happens, I'm as blind as a newborn pup, and that's exactly what happened when that pajama-suited nitwit ran out in front of me struttin' like he owned the swamp, tauntin' *take your best shot dingo girl!* Sure, I tore off after him . . . ran the little yuckster halfway down the ridge where he scrambled inside a hollow log half my size. I could stick my head in only so far—enough to see his *come and get me sucker!* grin. I cut loose a few high-pitched barks just to let the beady-eyed bugger know his string was runnin' out.

Then, quicker'n a bat flyin' out of a cypress beard, the candy-striper darted out the far end of the log and took off lickety-split down the Critter Trail toward the water. I knew full well I was s'posed to stay off that trail, that coyotes watched it all the time. How many times had Mama and my wild genes warned me it was courtin' disaster to even go near there? But

dumb me, I plumb forgot and chased off after the rabble rouser.
I was catchin' up, too, 'bout to nab his bushy tail, when in a
flash—

WHAM!

*Was that a gator log or the Phantom? Another bite or two and
I'd be gone.* The fear hit me 'fore I even felt the pain. But I never
heard a snarl and never felt a second chomp. Even so, a clang
and crunch echoed in my ears: the sound of steel on steel and
steel on bone. By then, a stabbin' pain was runnin' up and down
my front left leg, from my dew claw—the "thumb" I sometimes
use to chew bones—all the way up to my shoulder. When I
looked down, my sight was way too blurred to see what had me.
I was so woozy I could only tell that whatever grabbed me had
come from below my foot. Much as I hated pullin' up, I ever so
slightly lifted my leg. That caused shootin' pains that near 'bout
blacked me out. The burning and stabbing all seemed to come
from my left dew claw. I bent my head to give my left dew claw

WHAM! . . . I'm trapped by jaws of steel and licking blood around my
dew claw.

a lick. *Blood!* I licked that spot again and could tell then that my leg was cut to the bone. My foot was covered with matted leaves which I ever so slowly nosed aside. Now, I could see the trap with its jaws of steel—a spring-loaded trap used to catch critters, mainly coyotes.

By then the mornin' fog had lifted in more ways than one. It all came back: how Mama and I had seen a trapper sometime back settin' traps 'longside the Critter Trail. He chained 'em to small trees and covered 'em up with leaves. After that he had walked up the ridge draggin' a leg like it hurt bad. He sat down on a stump, lit up and watched the wind blowin' his smoke.

"Makin' sure the smoke's blowin' away from his trap," Mama whispered. "Can't have a critter sniffin' smoke and backin' off. You can see for yourself, chile, there's more'n one kinda gator log. The two-legged ones like him are the worst of all."

Next morning, after we saw that trapper, we heard a steel-jawed trap snap shut all the way up the hill in our den. It made a sickenin' sound. After a little while, Papa went down to check. When he came back, he told us a mama coyote was caught in the trap and strugglin' to break free.

"Got a litter of pups, too," Papa said, sadly shakin' his head.

"You saw 'em?" Mama asked.

"No, but I heard 'em cryin' in the bushes."

"What'll that poor mama do?"

"Won't surprise me if she tries to chew off her leg. How else can she get away?"

That shocked us pups no end. We stared at Papa for the longest time tryin' to take in what it meant. Glumly shakin' his head, he added, "If she does chew her leg off, the stump's gonna leave a trail of blood. That sorry trapper will follow every step she takes 'til he can shoot her and skin her hide."

We shivered all over when he said that.

I asked him what would happen to her pups.

"Let's not talk about that," was his grim reply.

9

Mama then put in sharply: "We've got enough to worry about just keepin' you pups safe. So 'member what your Papa said and stay off that Critter Trail!"

My trapped paw hurt even worse when I thought about that mama coyote tryin' to chew her leg off. Pretty soon a voice in my head started sayin' over and over: *Start chewin' your leg . . . Start chewin' your leg . . .* That's the last thing I 'member 'fore the pain made me pass out.

A strange dream followed where I saw myself stretched out under a bald cypress at the water's edge. The tree had plenty of knobby knees, or coneheads, stickin' up a foot or so above the waterline. I knew from what Papa said the knees are roots that hold the tree up. Its canopy's so big it takes a strong anchor to keep it right side up. Peepin' up like periscopes, the coneheads looked sorta dumb. Couldn't help but wonder if they got confused and just grew the wrong way.

Suddenly, a huge gator came swimmin' my way. It waded through the muck, crawled up the bank, opened its jaws, and flashed its teeth. Just as it started to chomp down, I heard a buzzin' sound and the gator's jaws locked up. It tried to bite me again and again, but each time its jaws got zapped. I noticed whiffs of smoke driftin' from the conehead tips. I was sure it had to be conehead mojo. It kept on zappin' and zappin' 'til the gator finally gave up and crawled away.

That told me the coneheads weren't so dumb after all. Somehow, they could beam safety rays all through the swamp. Papa had said many times that a great and mysterious force kept our bald cypress trees from gettin' sawed down. I could imagine a conehead zappin' a chainsaw just like it zapped the gator. Everybody knew the swamp wouldn't be the same without its dingos and bald cypress. "Keep on zappin'," I said aloud, thinkin' the force might hear me.

By then the hot August sun had burned off the mornin' fog and turned the trunks of the cypress trees burnt orange. A red-headed

10

woodpecker was peckin' away in a nearby gum tree—lookin' for carpenter ants, I s'posed. After a few rat-a-tats, he'd stop to look and then let go with a high piercin' call followed by a "luck . . . luck . . . luck" sound. I kept hopin' the woodpecker would draw attention to me, that somebody would come and get me outta the trap. I wondered why conehead mojo hadn't already saved me.

While I hoped and waited, I 'membered a poem Mama often told us at bedtime. A Mr. William Blake had wrote it, she said, to warn the wee ones, like us, to stay outta trouble. I could 'member every single word:

> My mother groaned, my father wept,
> Into the dangerous world I leapt.
> Helpless, naked, piping loud,
> Like a fiend hid in a cloud.

I dozed off wantin' to be a fiend hid in a cloud. I shudda' listened closer to Mama. If I'd done that, I'd never have stepped into a steel-jawed trap. Don't know how long I dozed, but I woke up in a place where I was even worse off than before.

3

Armed and Dangerous

"All I'm sayin' Topper Guy is careful what you trap."

"Well, she sure as hell ain't no sabertooth tiger."

"Maybe not, but she's dangered for sure, so I wouldn't shoot 'er."

"Dangered? Where'd that come from, Ragtop?"

"All I'm sayin' is you'd better check the dangered list."

"It ain't dangered, dumbo. It's *EN*-dangered—the Endangered List."

"I'm a-thinkin' she must be a red wolf."

"No chance of that and you know it. She's coyote all over."

"How come you're so sure? You ain't been trappin' all that long. Catch the wrong critter and the game warden's goin' to come down on you hard."

"Well, her pelt's goin' in the pile with all my other coyote skins."

"That ain't gonna fly either. Her coat's way too smooth—not rough and patchy. Bend down and take a whiff. She ain't got no odor at all. Better turn 'er loose and fore-git you ever saw 'er."

"Coulda done that back in the swamp. I brung 'er out so's you could look 'er over, Ragtop. Never figured on you bein' such a meathead."

"Hold on, I need another beer."

"Your brain's already turnin' to mush."

"Now ease up Topper Guy. I ain't goin' to rubber stamp everything you say."

They were kicked back in white plastic lawn chairs when I heard 'em talkin' 'bout me. Through a haze of rainbows and stars, I could trace the chain 'round my neck to the front porch rail of a rundown shack. Next, I looked down at my aching dew claw, all blue and caked with blood. A swarm of flies buzzed all 'round my wound and the blisterin' sun had 'em all riled up. At least the trap was gone, but what did that matter if this Topper Guy was gonna shoot me.

I was now thirsty enough to drink the Tugaloo River dry. 'Course the rowdies that trapped me hadn't bothered to put down a water bowl, let alone a food dish. I thought to myself: *That's the least you could do—especially for a dog on a chain.* Then I 'membered they didn't know what I was, which meant I had no rights at all. If they decided I was a coyote—well, I didn't even want to think about that.

A second, closer look at the shack told me it might be on the Endangered List too: swamp vines had nearly wrapped it up. I wondered where the blacktop road out front went. Aiken . . . Augusta . . . a crossroads country store? Out back a skiff with a small motor was tied to a rundown dock on a small reedy creek. My hunch was Topper Guy used the skiff to haul traps and whatever he caught in and outta the swamp.

He was a hard-eyed fellow with a stringy beard . . . wore hip waders and a gun shell vest. Didn't say much but aimed to have his way. His buddy Ragtop wore a greasy white bandana with a rebel flag. Musta got named for that. Sported a sly fox tattoo on his arm. Told myself thinks he's a Swamp Fox like General Francis Marion, the greatest dodger of 'em all. All the critters in these parts—two-legged and otherwise—know 'bout him.

Had to be Topper Guy's shack 'cause a row of steel-jawed traps hung on the clapboard wall facin' me. A row of skins on boards stretched there too. Musta not bothered him that the shack's paint had long since peeled off, that beer and soda cans, plastic bags, and tires littered the yard, or that rust was eatin' holes in the tin roof. Our southern creepin' vine, kudzu, was growin' up the side and had wrapped around the old stone chimney. Kudzu wraps around fence posts, phone poles, trees, and even old folks, I s'pose, if they don't get up and move around. It seemed the shack coulda been a country store 'cause it had a lot of rustin' signs of people drinkin' Coca-Cola and blowin' clouds of smoke. Lemme just say I *can* read pictures.

When Topper Guy hobbled over to get two more cans of beer from a cooler on the porch, it suddenly hit me I'd seen that gait before. He was draggin' one leg just like the trapper Mama and I saw on the Critter Trail. My fur rose when I 'membered that.

Even so, I played possum. When he came back, I heard the tops on the cans go *pfzzz-CHU*. "Crap!" Ragtop muttered in disgust. When I peeped, he was wipin' foam from his face and dryin' his knuckles on his shirt.

"If she ain't a coyote, then what is she?" Topper Guy asked. Puttin' a foot on my belly, he pushed hard. I held my breath tight, but a low moan did slip out.

"I'm gittin' this over," he added. "I'm puttin' 'er down."

"You're takin' a mighty big chance. Better let 'er go."

"Just hand me the gun Ragtop. I can't stand varmints anyway. My aim is to clear every last one outta the swamp."

I'd seen a double-barreled shotgun next to the cooler. Ragtop drained his beer, tossed the can in the bushes, and slowly rose from his chair.

That's when the voice in my head said, *Run fool run! . . . Make a break for it while you can!* My muscles tensed as I tried to get on my feet, but I just couldn't move. I was too weak. Besides, with only three legs to run on, how far could I get? The voice in my head piped up again, *If you can't run, then plead. Look pitiful and sad.*

But no way could I do that. No way could I let Knucklehead and Trigger-happy make me beg. I saw Topper Guy open the gun and put a shell in each barrel . . . saw him snap the barrels into place . . . and watched him aim straight at me. I rolled over then and turned my back, knowin' the worst was about to come.

Just wish I'd listened to what Mama said.

I closed my eyes and waited . . . but then—

"Better hold on, Topper Guy. Someone's a-comin'."

I could also hear a car and not far off at all. As it slowed, its tires crunched the gravel out front. I rolled over and saw a shiny black truck stoppin' in front the shack.

"Put that up," Topper Guy said, handin' his gun back to Ragtop.

"Friend of yours drivin' that?" Ragtop asked.

Topper Guy's eyebrows arched like a cat's stretch. "The dudes I know don't drive rigs like that," he said.

A pretty woman got out of the truck and made a beeline for me. She wore a pink blouse, a dark blue skirt, and tall black boots. Her crow-colored hair and dark glasses gave her a mysterious look. *Just in time*, I told myself. *No way will they try to cross her.*

4

My Hide Gets Saved

Before the pretty lady got within earshot, Topper Guy told Ragtop to grab a burlap bag from behind the chairs and cover me up. Once that was done, I couldn't see a lick, but my antenna ears were workin' overtime. They heard the tall black boots comin' closer and closer.

"Anything we can do for you?" Topper Guy asked in a mealy-mouthed way.

A soothin' voice replied: "I was just passing through and thought I'd stop by to ask if either one of you gentlemen have seen any vagrant dogs?"

"Vagrant! That some kinda breed?"

"No, it just means they're homeless. Most call the dogs I'm looking for American Dingos or sometimes the Yellow Dog. Have you by chance seen one?"

"No ma'am, we haven't, but we wouldn't know one if we did."

"They're mighty special dogs. Wonderful pets. You even hear them called strays, but that, too, is incorrect; the proper term is feral."

"FUR-al?" Ragtop asked. I knew dern well he didn't have the slightest idea what that meant. But then, neither did I.

"Feral means wild, but even that's misleading. They just happen to live in wild places like the swamp. They're actually a registered breed known as the Carolina Dog. I prefer American Dingos because they live in the Deep South."

"Well, we ain't seen none," Topper Guy said.

"By the way, I'm Jane—Jane Gunnell. Would you mind giving me a call if you do see one?"

"Reckon we can do that." Topper Guy soft-soaped her.

"Take my card and let me be on my way. I've still got a lot of ground to cover."

Suddenly it hit me. I'd better start wigglin' fast—do anything I could to get the pretty lady's attention. I began thumpin' my tail hard.

She musta seen the bag move 'cause I heard straight off, "What's under that bag? It must be alive. Let me see what's there!"

"Nothin'," Ragtop replied. "Nothin' you need to be worryin' 'bout."

"Strange—do you mind if I take a peek?"

At that, Topper Guy snapped: "Now you're buttin' in lady and we don't 'preciate that one bit."

Just then my tail slipped out from under the bag.

"I *thought* so," Miss Jane exclaimed. "I want to see for myself." I could feel her kneelin' beside me and pullin' the burlap bag back. The voice in my head ordered, *Give 'er the saddest look you've got.*

I s'pose I did 'cause her hand instantly flew to her mouth and she cried out in shock: "Poor baby! What have they done to you?"

"Ain't done nothin' yet," Topper Guy objected. "We were fixin' to turn 'er loose just as you drove up."

"My god—in this scorching heat you covered her up?" She lifted the bag with two fingers like some skunk had sprayed it good. "Can't you see that she's suffocating?"

"We were tryin' to keep the sun off'n her," Topper Guy offered feebly.

"It was the onliest way we could do that," Ragtop chipped in.

Miss Jane ran her hand down my back gently and gave me several caring pats. "Don't shake, sweetheart—no one will hurt you now."

"Feel how hot she is," she demanded. "She's burning up and desperate for a drink of water." She had patted my head and was runnin' her hand down my back when she caught sight of my dew claw. Snatchin' her sunglasses off, she leaned down for a closer look, and all the color drained out'n her face.

"This poor baby's been trapped!" she exclaimed.

My captors gave her dumb looks. "So, what if she was," Topper Guy said with a shrug.

Miss Jane arrives in the nick of time—a trapper is going to shoot me.

"She's an American Dingo—the very kind of dog I'm looking for. You told me you hadn't seen one."

"We thought she might be a red wolf," Ragtop put in. "Somethin' on the dangered list."

"She's in danger from the heat. This puppy needs help."

"We 'preciate your concern ma'am," Topper Guy stiffly replied. "But we can handle this by ourself. We sure don't need any help from the likes of you."

"Maybe not, but I want to take her home with me. I give dogs like her a place to live and the loving care they need."

"You keep on callin' her a dog," Topper Guy objected. "She ain't a dog—she's a coyote pure and simple."

"I can assure you that this sweet young thing is an American Dingo. I ought to know because I breed American Dingos."

"Well, we ain't never seen one before."

Ragtop then stepped in with a threat: "We ain't got no use for meddlers. I'm gittin' the gun."

"Stay put dumb ass," Topper Guy growled.

"I'm more than willing to leave," Miss Jane said calmly. "But I have to take the dog with me. She needs immediate care and attention."

"Look here ma'am, I'm a trapper and my time's gotta be worth somethin'."

"I don't question that for a moment."

"You gotta admit that I did bring 'er out of the swamp. I'm makin' the best I can of a bad situation."

"If you want to make the best of it, let me have the dog."

"I still think she's a coyote and I git fifty bucks for one of their hides."

"Fifty dollars, will that make this right as far as you're concerned?"

"I'm thinkin' just maybe it would."

"Then I'll go get my purse. Just leave this poor baby right where she is."

I could see how mad Miss Jane was from the way she flounced back to her truck.

Ragtop let out a low whistle as she walked away. "The boys at Scooter's would be mighty impressed if I rode up in that land yacht with her."

"You ain't ridin' nowhere with her," Topper Guy shot back. "That woman's big trouble. I want to get her outta here—and now!"

When Miss Jane came back, she had the money in one hand and a plastic water bottle in the other. She gave the money to Topper Guy and asked Ragtop to find a container I could drink from.

Ragtop hurried off and soon came back with a plastic beer cup. Miss Jane filled it and helped me to my feet. I slurped the water down as fast as I could.

"Easy sweetheart. You can have all the wah-wah you want."

Didn't know what wah-wah was but loved the way she said it. I splashed a bit on her blouse 'cause I couldn't drink it fast enough. It felt like I was drainin' the Tugaloo River dry as I drank from that cup.

Once I finished, she picked me up and cradled me in her arms. It was my first chance to lick her nose. She didn't seem to mind one bit, so I licked it again.

"Want me to take 'er to the car for you?" Ragtop asked.

"Thank you but I'll do that myself."

When we got to the truck, she put me down on the seat, which felt soft and cushy. I looked up then into her eyes. They were warm and caring. No one, 'ceptin' Mama, had ever looked at me like that before.

After tellin' me I might fall off the seat, she pulled a strap around me and snapped it into a holder. It clicked like the barrels of Topper Guy's shotgun snappin' into place. I told myself right then and there that I hoped I'd never see another gun.

"Relax sweetie. No one's going to harm you—not when you're with me."

She started the truck, turned around, and drove off. Couldn't believe how fast she went. The car was twice as fast as anyone I'd seen on the Critter Trail. My first time on wheels, and in what Ragtop had called a land yacht, no less.

Miss Jane's just-in-time rescue was more'n plain luck. I was sure the coneheads had beamed out a safety ray to her. How else could I have been saved from a steel-jawed trap or Topper Guy's gun?

'Course that didn't mean I'd get off, as the swamp elders said, scratch free. Topper Guy was madder'n a wet hornet when we left. Miss Jane had out-talked him—backed him down and paid him off, too. That had to give him the slow burn. She'd lit his fuse, and sooner or later he'd go off like a stick of dynamite. If he got half a chance to shoot me, he wouldn't dawdle the next time. Coyote, Yeller Dog, American Dingo, Carolina Dog—they were all fair game to Topper Guy. He meant every word of it when he told Ragtop he'd clear the swamp of every last one of us if it was the last thing he did. Then it hit me: Could my pack in the swamp be next?

5

I Get Named

I felt sooo grateful to Miss Jane for gettin' the best of Topper Guy and whiskin' me away from that creepin' kudzu shack of his on Timm's Creek. That was the name, accordin' to her, of the stream out back. When she let me lick her nose, I wanted to tell her in the worst way what a sorry skunk Topper Guy was, how he was fixin' to shoot me just as she drove up. I was turnin' myself inside out over how to tell her we hadn't seen the last of him. I knew he'd trap or shoot my pack and the whole dingo tribe if he got half a chance.

Somehow, I had to find a way to get that point across. Somehow, I had to get her to ask the right question. Then, I could thump my tail hard and she'd know how that meant "yes." If I just sat quiet as a mouse, she'd know my answer was "no." I thought a sad look—like I'd just lost my best friend—would tell her I wanted her to ask somethin' else.

Soon as we got to the main road, Miss Jane went in the Piggly Wiggly store and came out with a bag full of stuff. She carried me to a patch of grass and began doctorin' my dew claw. First, she poured water from a bottle on these little cotton balls and washed all over the dew claw as best she could. Then she opened up another bottle that looked like water, too, but this time when she poured, I thought my dew claw had caught on fire. I let out a a bunch of yelps. "Alcohol," she told me and blew on my dew claw to make the fire go out. Never did see any sign of fire but worried it might blaze up at any moment. Once my hurt started to go away, she wrapped my leg in a see-through cloth and covered it over with a sticky tape.

"That will have to do until I can get you to Dr. Rumley—he's our vet. Chances are your leg is broken and he'll have to set it and put it in a cast." She said I'd been so good I deserved a treat. "You must be starving, so how about some Purina Chow with real chicken?" She opened a small tube and pinched off a piece the size of her thumb. She let me sniff it and I could tell straight off it'd be downright delicious. Just then she held a pinch out in front of my nose. I was so hungry I snapped it out of her fingers. "Dummy," I told myself. "That way you'll never get any more."

After that I let her put each piece on my tongue before I gulped it down. I even got to lick the smell off her fingers. Wow! Redbone smelled good and tasted even better—way better'n snake or grub. One by one Miss Jane fed me every last bit from the tube. What more could I ask for?

Next, she drove me to Dr. Rumley's. He was an older man in a white coat. When he saw my leg, he said "tut-tut." Shakin' his head, he told Miss Jane: "Sorry to say but it's definitely broken, but with proper care, it should mend just fine." Then, 'fore I knew it, he stuck a needle in my hiney. I let out my worst howl 'cause it was worse'n any nip I ever got from Mama. He then put a cast on me from the top of my paw and dew claw near to the top of my left shoulder. "Now, be a good girl," he said, "and don't go chewing on your cast because it needs to last until your leg heals." Just to be safe he fastened a big cone around my neck. "That should do it," he told me.

After we got back in the truck, I tried my derndest to get around that cone and chew off the cast. But the cone wouldn't let me. Miss Jane told me, "You're going to be just fine once I take

24

you home to Banbury Cross Farm. You'll be safe there and won't have to worry about those trappers ever again. Ready to go?"

I thumped my tail as hard as I could. It was my first chance to say yes and leave no doubt about what I meant. Even so I still was worried—real worried—'bout what Topper Guy might do next. He was bound to set more traps along the Critter Trail. Someone was sure to get caught, and it could be Mama, Papa, Sugar, or Popeye (my sister and brother). Even worse they might get shot. Somehow I had to tell Miss Jane 'cause I knew she'd save my pack if she could.

"One not-so-small problem," she told me. "You've got to have a name. Your face is adorable—which is why I keep calling you sweetie. Surely, we can find something more descriptive than sweetie. What about Dingo Dolly . . . or Dingo Molly? Maybe Brownie for your deep brown searching eyes. Sweetie fits your disposition just perfectly. What else is sweet? . . . Honeybees . . . honeybee sweet. That's it! Honey! . . . Honey's perfect, and it's also the color of your coat. Why didn't I think of that first? Are you happy with the name Honey? Is it okay for me to call you Honey?"

I thumped out a happy yes 'cause that name sounded just perfect to me.

We soon turned into a lovely gravel lane arched over by live oaks full of Spanish moss. Just as we turned, she pointed to a sign above the road. "See that? It says, 'Banbury Cross Farm—Home of Man's Best Friends.'"

A moment later a bunch of dogs—way more'n a pack—came runnin' toward us from both sides of the road. "You're about to meet your new brothers and sisters," Miss Jane said. "I'm sure they'll give you a very warm welcome." I couldn't believe my eyes: every last one of 'em had antenna ears and fishhook tails like mine. They'd all been saved from swamps along the Savannah River. She laughed and gave my ears a rub. "Just love your ears.

Bet you can pick up Radio Moscow, maybe even signals from outer space." I couldn't even guess what that meant.

She told me the American Dingos were 'bout to become extinct. "That means disappear as in *forever*," she added. "I couldn't let that happen, so I decided to set up a rescue squad. We ride out to lots of remote places searching for dogs like you who need a good home. You'll be meeting the rest of the rescue squad shortly."

I'd never seen a house like hers. It sat dead center at the end of that long lane leading in from the blacktop—a big white house with tall columns in front. Right away I knew Miss Jane had to be crazy 'bout flowers—it looked like a rainbow got planted in her yard. A pot of gold too 'cause it looked like the perfect place to live. Everywhere I looked flower beds, shapely bushes, and window boxes were bloomin' rainbow colors. Across from the house as we drove in, I saw a large fenced-in pasture and horses grazin'. A big red barn sat just inside the fence with bales of hay stacked neatly nearby. Behind the house, where she parked the truck, a wide green lawn sloped down to a pond where geese were swimmin' without a care in the world. It was then that I caught sight of a row of dog houses on the side of the house opposite the barn. They were painted bright colors and had a name above each door. When she saw me takin' all this in, she told me, "That's Champion's Row. Gypsy, Buttons, Fax, and Snipper all live here, and the biggest house of all is for our grand champion, Pockets."

She opened the truck door and, once again, gathered me in her arms. I figured she'd take me to one of the pens where the other dogs stayed—that I'd stay there 'til my leg healed and I could walk and run. Instead, she carried me up the back steps and straight into the house. Put me in a basket right beside the kitchen table.

"Now Honey, I want you to stay right here until your leg heals. You need a lot of rest and a lot of T-L-C. Do you know about TLC? It stands for tender loving care."

I thumped my tail as hard as I could when she said that 'cause I really, really wanted her to love me.

The wicker basket she put me in was snug when I curled up. I was drowsy, so I closed my eyes and nodded off thinkin' how lucky I was to land in Miss Jane's arms. I had a new home and a new name. I liked Honey . . . it made me think of all the bees buzzin' in her yard with all those rainbow colors.

But once I fell asleep, I had a terrible dream. Miss Jane was prunin' azaleas and I was dreamin' and whimperin' in the grass close by. I was sure Miss Jane would wake me and ask if I was dreamin' about Topper Guy. Once she did, I aimed to get on my feet, take a few steps, and fall dead (play-actin', that is). I figured that would tell her Topper Guy wanted to shoot me and my pack, too.

But for some reason Miss Jane couldn't hear me. She just kept on prunin' azaleas. I was beside myself 'cause I knew, somehow, time was runnin' out. The only thing I could do was thump my tail over and over, but Miss Jane never even noticed that. Suddenly, from nowhere, I saw Topper raise his gun and aim it at Mama. Then I heard myself screamin': *Stop him! Stop him! He's gonna shoot my Mama!*

6

Alpha Moms

Someone shook me, shook me hard. Then I heard the concerned voice of Miss Jane: "Wake up Honey! Wake up little girl; you're having a bad dream."

I realized then that I was safe and snug in my wicker basket and that sorry roach, Topper Guy, hadn't shot Mama after all. Can't tell you how relieved I was, but even so, I was shakin' from head to toe. Miss Jane was kneelin' on the floor beside me, slowly strokin' my back, slowly calmin' my nerves. What a crazy dream for her not to see or hear me. Whenever I needed her, she was always there. I could never do without her. Later, I learned that she was just like Mama—an Alpha Mom.

Someone had to 'splain to me what an alpha mom is, that they don't get the respect they deserve and aren't even known about by many. I was told I'd hear plenty about alpha males: how strong they are, how great they are for protection. The alpha male is Number One and no one else comes close. That rubs me the wrong way. The alpha mom is very strong too—she just happens to use her strength in ways you might never see. When I heard all this, I knew my Mama and Miss Jane were like two peas in a pod—they were both alpha moms.

Lemme just say a dingo can't survive without his or her alpha mom. In our tribe, Mama is Number One and don't you dare to cross her. She runs the pack with love pats and tough cuffs. When it comes to predators, she aims not to fight 'em off, but to make dern sure they never find the den or her pups. To accomplish this, Papa has to bend his will to hers. I've seen her command him with nothin' but a stern look, a low growl, or by puttin' her paw on his neck. They may be small signs, but they leave no doubt on who's boss.

Just before our litter was born, Mama dug a large cone-shaped hole and gave birth to us there. She took us in and out of the hole daily—always by the scruff of the neck while keepin' a close watch for predators. We left the hole for good after five weeks and moved to a den Papa had built in the crotch of a black gum tree. It was a barrel-sized lean-to under the gum's clay-covered roots. Its leak-proof roof was made of branches and leaves mixed with clay. It kept us warm and dry even in the worst of storms.

After we got weaned, Mama still made sure we all ate right. Each day she and Papa would go out to find grubs, voles, lizards, and frogs to eat. When they came back to the den, they'd heave it all up so we could chow down on their partly digested food. That was easier and much safer too since we didn't have to go outside where an owl, a chicken hawk, or a coyote could snatch us in the blink of an eye.

Mama allowed no pup to start squealin' cause that could give the den away. When a squealer tuned up, she took it by the head in her mouth and gave it a good shake. That stopped the racket quick and told the little rascal to respect his or her elders. Another lesson was—be careful where you poop. Poopin' in the den is a big no-no and draws a hard cuff to the head. Failin' to cover poop outside draws another hard smack. Mama also taught us to lick our bodies clean to cut down on smell and sheddin'. She aimed to raise little phantoms: pups that couldn't be heard, smelled, or tracked. With our marsh grass–colored coats, we were 'bout as hard to see as phantoms.

The peckin' order of the pack comes clear at snake-killin' time. Mama gathers the pack in a circle 'round the snake and feints

30

with a paw to make it crawl. Once it does, she or Papa grabs the snake's tail and gives it a whip-like snap that breaks its neck. I learned how to do that at about one year old.

Ace, Miss Jane's farm manager, told me a story one day that helped me see there's more'n one kind of alpha mom. He'd let me come inside his Airstream, a sausage-shaped house trailer, and the niftiest contraption I'd ever seen. He called it the Clipper 'cause it was designed by Charles Lindberg, the first person to fly across some ocean. Ace ate lunch in the Clipper and slept there when he stayed at the farm. While he ate lunch, he'd cut thin hot dog slices and feed 'em to me. Naturally, I couldn't wait to go inside when Ace said, "We need to talk in private."

Ace told me, "Miss Jane's tough as nails, but no one can talk dingo like she can. She knows just how sensitive you are—how you'll shun anyone who speaks in a harsh or ugly way. And lordy, lordy, don't ever try usin' a heavy hand. Anyone who tries that could get a serious tongue lashin'.

Ace takes care of the farm and me too.

31

Ace was right. Miss Jane *could* speak dingo. Her voice had a soft musical tone that made me want to climb right up in her lap. Ace had once joked, "Honey, how come you keep fallin' for all that baby talk? Did your mama talk to you like that?" Didn't know what that was, but if Miss Jane was servin' it, it was good enough for me.

I loved what Miss Jane called her "terms of endearment." She only spoke to me in her sing-song way when no one else could hear us. She could string words together to beat the band: "funny bunny, pointy-eared pointer, brown-eyed baby" and the like. I talked right back with my eyes: "brown pools of mystery," she called 'em. She often said I used more body language than she did. The fur on my neck would rise when I was scared, my tail wagged when I was happy, and I licked a face or nose when I wanted to say, "I love you."

I often wondered what made me special to Miss Jane. Every dingo in the kennel adored her. Give any one of 'em half a chance and it'd jump straight into my wicker basket. But one day she answered the question for me: "What I love about you Honey is your courage and pluck. You hardly whimpered when your leg was broken. You've got true dingo grit, girl."

Ace also told me in the Clipper that Miss Jane came from a famous family—lots of lawyers, politicians, and bigwigs. "Coulda had a life of ease," Ace said, "but she rolled up her sleeves and went to work when she learned your breed was about to vanish. She began to scour country roads and back roads in the swamps to find and save every dingo she could."

Ace also said she'd helped define what the perfect dingo ought to look like startin' with our antenna ears. Folks may laugh at how they stick up, but they do that for a reason: we hear lots of sounds others miss. Sometimes we tune in by bendin' one ear forward while the other rotates in search of sounds. Another feature that sets us apart is a deep "V" chest and tucked up loin that gives us our sturdy look. But nothin' stands out more than our fishhook tail. We use it to talk, especially on a hunt. When it's forty-five degrees below horizontal we're searching for prey. If it sinks lower or drops between our legs, then we're worried, ashamed, or afraid, and when it's in a fishhook shape, we're on high alert. These positions signal to the pack whether we're trackin', closin' in, or ready to pounce on some prey.

Color also defines the perfect dingo. Mine, as Miss Jane said, is the same as honey—just what it ought to be. She says my coat is tinged straw-brown with a hint of orange or ginger. I also have white feathering on my throat, belly, and backside. A few dingos have plain red coats or cream-colored coats with brown spots. In the autumn, when the leaves fall, I blend in with the colors so well you have to look close to see me. As she bred dingos over the years, Miss Jane worked hard to bring out all our special traits—the fine points of our genes that may make us, as I've already said, the oldest breed in North America.

As an alpha mom, Miss Jane had turned many of her dingos into champions. Two of her dogs, Star and Saigon, had been Master Champions of the American Rare Breed Association. Others had won obedience and herding titles. In addition, her dogs had swept the field in agility trials with performances that were among the best ever posted in events requiring split-second timing and incredible jumpin' skills. She had a wall full of trophies and ribbons to prove beyond any doubt that her methods worked. Finally, she decided she'd proved her point and stopped showing dingos herself and began working with those she'd placed dogs with to help them win trophies and championships.

Despite all her trophies and ribbons, as well as the demands of running a successful kennel, Miss Jane always found time for me. In our own little world, she'd tell me I had "perky, perfect ears" . . . that my ears were "two jibs on a boat blowing in the wind." That made me feel so special and pumped my chest full of pride.

It makes me very happy and proud to know that I've got two different kinds of alpha moms doin' all they can to keep our breed from vanishin'. One is four-legged, and one is just two, but I love 'em both just the same.

7

I Land in a Clump of Clover

Once I got to Banbury Cross Farm, I couldn't help but feel like I got throwed in a clump of clover. No wonder! My wicker basket was safe and comfy and it made my narrow escape seem far, far away. Then, too, somethin' cookin' on the stove smelled downright delicious. Not far from my nose two brown leather boots rose like a pair of live oaks. A tall, fine-lookin' gentleman of about fifty was standin' at the stove in his socks. He had a high forehead, curious eyes, and brown hair combed straight back just like the Swamp Fox combed his. From Miss Jane's description on the ride to the farm, it had to be Mr. Billy. He had the newspaper spread out nearby and was tappin' on his thigh with a long-handled fork.

He soon spied my eyes fixed on him. "Top o' the morning young lass. Hear you had rather a rough time of it yesterday. Miss Jane will be back shortly. She instructed me to cook you a tasty breakfast snack." He stuck the long-handled fork in a pan and lifted out somethin' long, thin, and bubbly. "Just the morsel to start your day off right—a fine strip of bacon." He dangled it 'til it cooled, broke off a piece, and held it just above my nose.

Dumb hungry me! Wouldn't you know for the second time I snapped without thinkin' and came close to chompin' his fingers? "Easy girl," he laughed. "You can have some more." My first bite of bacon was sooo good. Soon as it went down, I told myself, *that's even better'n the treat Miss Jane gave me.* After giving me a few more pieces, Mr. Billy put a water bowl on the floor next to my basket. I tried gettin' up but couldn't. I'd forgot all about the cast. Mr. Billy reached down, picked me up, and lowered me 'til my feet touched the floor. I was shaky and the leg in the cast hurt when I put the slightest bit of weight on it. Mr. Billy held me while I drank, then put me back in the basket and gave my cast a friendly pat. Just then, we heard a car drivin' up and he said, "Honey, I'm reminded at this very moment of those great lines from *Romeo and Juliet*—

Mr. Billy's strip of bacon is way better than anything I ever tasted in the swamp.

He jests at scars, that never felt a wound,
But soft! what light through yonder window
breaks?
It is the east, and Juliet is the sun!

Just then Miss Jane came into the kitchen and Mr. Billy winked at me. "What did I tell you, Honey? Juliet is here after all. Lest there be any doubt, our Juliet is Miss Jane."

"Seems that I've heard that line before," Miss Jane laughed and put her things on the counter. "Has Mr. Billy been quoting Shakespeare to you, Honey? He's always quoting the Bard or Longfellow or maybe even some short fellow—just depends on what comes into his head at the time. He'd have you believe he's a man of letters."

Never heard of a man of letters or the Bard, but I especially liked what Mr. Billy said 'bout jestin' at scars 'cause I felt my wound to be no jokin' matter. I was curious how Miss Jane and Mr. Billy jested with each other—they reminded me of pups in the den cuffin' each other. Instead of paws they used fancy words. Made me wonder how I'd ever learn what was really goin' on at Banbury Cross Farm and how long I'd get to stay.

After breakfast I learned that not only did Mr. Billy comb his hair like my favorite dodger, he rode a horse like the Swamp Fox too. He carried me outside and put me—basket and all—in a wheelbarrow which he pushed across the road to the stables. "Time for you to meet O'Malley," he said. "Wait here while I go inside the stall and tack up. In case you don't know, 'tack up' means to saddle up and get ready to ride." When he led O'Malley out, I could hardly believe my eyes: the horse was a giant with a smooth brown coat just a-ripplin' with muscles. I s'posed he'd have to be huge to carry a man the size of Mr. Billy.

"We'll take a short exercise run," he said in mountin', and off they went at a slow, easy pace. 'Fore long they were gallopin' across the paddock at breakneck speed. Then, suddenly, they headed for a short piece of fence. I thought they'd stop, but Mr. Billy leaned forward against O'Malley's neck and the horse soared up and over the top rail with room to spare. Amazin' how Mr. Billy and O'Malley seemed to be one and the same as they thundered across that field. The practice run, I later learned, was for a big fox hunt comin' up in a few days.

Big fox hunts and expert horsemen were nothin' new to Aiken. Mr. Billy said the town had been the home of the horsey for a century because so many people brought horses there for foxhunts. By the late 1800s rich folks were comin' south to ride in balmy weather and socialize. They formed a "Winter Colony" and Aiken soon became the polo capital of the United States. Hitchcock Woods, which got named for a war hero, was the center of it all.

The hero was Tommy Hitchcock Jr., who ran off as a teenager and joined the Lafayette Flying Corps in France during World War I. He got shot down and captured by the Germans but escaped by jumpin' from a movin' train. During World War II he convinced military leaders to build the P-51 Mustang, a bomber escort that helped win the air war in Europe. But just before the war ended, he met with a tragic end: his Mustang nosedived during a test flight and he never could pull out. He and his sister had donated the land for Hitchcock Woods which stands today as one of the largest urban forests in America.

In the 1950s the US government put a top-secret bomb plant in Aiken to make nukes for the Cold War. It employed thousands of high-paid workers and changed the place from a waterin' hole for the wealthy to more of a middle-class town. "The horse lost some of its influence after that," Mr. Billy said. "It was an odd mix of steeplechases and polo matches side-by-side with Harry homeowners and Little League baseball games."

While Mr. Billy gave O'Malley a rubdown and a big bag of oats, Miss Jane pushed me back across the road to meet the dingos she'd rescued and see my friend, Ace, who took me inside his

Airstream and fed me those delicious hot dog slices. She took treats—usually a sack full of day-old bread—on each visit, so naturally the dingos jumped with joy at the sight of her. There musta been two dozen or so dogs in the kennel, but she patiently broke off pieces of bread for each one. Once she'd finished her rounds she went back to the house—"to catch up on calls and correspondence"—leavin' me with Ace.

After she left, he told me, "That woman thinks you're the cat's meow. You're stayin' in the Big House. Even the champions don't get to stay there." 'Course they all had nice houses out back which I'd seen. "The regular folks all stay with me," Ace said.

Wasn't sure what regular folks meant, but I could see that the dingos inside the kennel all loved Ace. He did special things to make them comfy—like fillin' blue plastic tubs with water so they could douse, dunk, and cool. I learned that he and Miss Jane had worked together for over ten years and shared a great affection for all their dogs.

"She's the Outside and I'm the Inside," Ace told me. That meant Miss Jane met with people who wanted a dingo and sized them up. In the meantime, Ace fed and watered the dogs, made sure their pens were clean, and doctored any dog that happened to get sick. He also ordered supplies and kept track of all kinds of stuff.

Ace was the first black man I'd ever met. He'd played pro football as a young man and had the broad shoulders and thick neck to prove it. Also said he'd wanted to be a boxer like some famous champion. Can't quite 'member his name, but it might a-been Mahatma Ali. Although he never got in the ring, Ace got his nose broke in football so many times it pointed off to one side. "Got cauliflower jar lids too," he told me foldin' down a ear.

Not long after I arrived, he said, "Miss Honey, let me tell you there's something special about all God's creatures. What I see in you is heart—a mighty big heart for a girl not yet

39

two years old. I'm mighty glad Miss Jane saved you from that Sidewinder." By Sidewinder I was pretty sure he meant the trapper Topper Guy.

My chest puffed out just a bit when I heard that, but I still missed my family more'n I let on. I knew Topper Guy would be settin' traps up and down the Critter Trail—that any of my pack could get caught just like I did. If so, who'd save their hides? There was nothin' worse'n gettin' trapped—not even heart worms. I wanted the pack safe—safe as I was at Banbury Cross Farm. I had been so lucky that conehead mojo had throwed me in a briar patch, a place that felt like home, one where dingos were treated mighty special, too. The closer I got to Miss Jane, Mr. Billy, and Ace, the more I felt like I had a new pack.

But could I have two? "Never forget, the pack comes first—*always!*" Mama and Papa had told me that for as long as I could 'member. I had to be loyal always, could never forget 'em, not for one moment. Suddenly it came to me that surely a pack could grow—that Miss Jane, Mr. Billy, and Ace *were* my second pack now. After what they'd done for the dingos, they'd left no doubt that they were *all for one and one for all,* which is what the pack is all about.

For the first time I began to see that we *were* all one big pack 'cause we'd stick together through thick and thin. I could put my trust in Miss Jane, Mr. Billy, and Ace just like I did in the pack that raised me. I just wished we could be together now. I had a hole inside my heart and knew it'd never be filled 'til I saw Mama, Papa, Sugar, and Popeye again.

Still, I loved Miss Jane for doctorin' my dew claw and feedin' me that Redbarn Natural Beef. I loved Mr. Billy for his quotin', even for how he combed his hair, and I 'specially loved Ace for the way he could make each and every dingo feel so special. Seemed to me I could love my family in the swamp and love my family at Banbury Cross Farm at one and the same time. I 'membered what Ace said—that I had a mighty big heart for a girl not yet two years old.

Later that day I heard Mr. Billy tellin' Miss Jane that two trappers had been braggin' at a hangout called Scooter's Bar and Eats 'bout snookerin' her in a dog deal. They were laughin' at how dumb she was to pay fifty dollars for a ditch dog.

"The way Ace tells it they're certain they bamboozled you," Mr. Billy told her.

"Let them think what they want; it doesn't matter to me at all," she replied. "I got everything I could have hoped for in little Miss Honey."

Couldn't have been happier to hear that. Even so, I couldn't help worrying about what Topper Guy had said, "Ditch dogs all happen to be varmints—and they all gotta go." But I decided not to let that get me down. Miss Jane and Mr. Billy and Ace had brought me into a whole new world full of excitin' adventures. I couldn't help but wonder what would come next.

8

Wide, Wide World

The followin' day I got my first history lesson, and it wasn't one bit borin' either. After breakfast Miss Jane wrapped a fresh bandage around my dewclaw and hugged me close around the neck. She promised my leg would be good as new in no time at all.

"The two of us have lots of exploring to do," she said with a knowing smile. "There's a wide, wide world out there for you to discover, but it won't make much sense unless you know a lot more about a subject—what we call the past—that we mustn't overlook."

When she mentioned explorin', I figured we'd go pokin' 'bout the farm. I still hadn't seen the ducks and geese, but Ace had warned me not to chase 'em 'cause I'd be sure to land in hot water if I did. Turned out that Miss Jane wasn't talkin' 'bout explorin' the farm at all. She aimed to look back at my story in particular. Seemed like a strange idea. I'd never given any thought at all to who I was or where I came from. How'd I come to live in the swamp? Well, hadn't thought about that either. As it turned out, Miss Jane opened my eyes to a world I never even knew was there—what she called "The noble history of your tribe."

She first took me down the hall to the Champion's Room where the walls were lined with photos and ribbons—mostly blue—of famous dogs raised at Banbury Cross Farm. One in particular—Pockets—had won many championships in agility. I was amazed by how much we all looked alike. The dogs whose photos lined the walls had all been found in swamps along the Savannah River or had been born on the farm.

"Just wanted you to see firsthand, Honey, that you belong to a mighty special breed.

You're an American Dingo or Carolina Dog, which are one and the same. There's a strong possibility that yours is the oldest breed in North America, that you are direct descendants of the wolf. Your ancestors crossed the Bering Strait when there was a land bridge between what's now Russia and Alaska. They arrived many centuries before the Europeans came."

Mr. Billy came in and sat down on the couch with us. He heard most of what Miss Jane said and added, "What's so wonderful about the dingos is that you haven't been overbred like the dogs the Europeans brought. Through all those centuries in the wilds, you bred naturally and developed unique traits to avoid

My ancestors on the Trail of Tears jump into the icy waters of the Mississippi to follow the Native Americans across.

predators. That's how you came to have so little odor. Because an American Dingo leaves no scent, you're almost impossible to track."

What they said sounded mighty grand, but I really didn't feel that special. I wondered if they knew how it was to live in the wild, to get called bad names, and to even get shot at with a gun. My feelings were hurt when someone called me a "no-account stray." Their tone of voice said they didn't want me around and might even think I was dangerous. What hurt worst of all was to get called a "ditch dog." Sounded like the lowest form of life on earth, one that ought to be wiped out. I got called that mainly when people saw me sittin' in the roadside ditch lilies which were the color of my coat. Don't mind sayin' I favored such spots 'cause food often got tossed from cars, and if I kept my eyes peeled, I could have fries and nuggets, even burger bites.

Musta had a sad look on my face 'cause Mr. Billy asked Miss Jane if he'd hurt my feelings. "I hope not," he added. "When I see her sweet face, I think of the Garden of Eden where her ancestors once lived. That may have been the last time man truly lived in harmony with nature. The Native Americans said they could see god in a dingo's deep brown eyes. Did you know that, Honey?"

Miss Jane told me Mr. Billy was President of the Edgefield County Historical Society—that he'd done lots of research on the Cherokee Indians and their dogs. He showed me a picture of a great Cherokee Chief named Dragging Canoe who had fought at the time of the Revolutionary War to keep white settlers from takin' more and more Cherokee land. But Mr. Billy said it was a losing battle 'cause "ambitious politicians and ruthless swindlers kept on gobblin' up Indian lands. They took it any way they could."

To hear Mr. Billy tell it, seemed like my breed had been with the Indians a lot longer than anyone could say. We showed up in drawings more'n two hundred years ago. "There was no one Indian dog," Mr. Billy told me, "but no other breed shows up as often as your dingo and Carolina Dog ancestors. I especially like the pictures of them pulling a travois." Had no idea what that was, but he 'splained it was a sled with two poles we dragged across the ground. Better'n a wheel, he said, especially in the woods or on snowy ground. We musta had tools, food, and other stuff tied to the top of those poles.

"Ever hear of the Trail of Tears?" Mr. Billy asked. "Most people think only the Cherokees and other tribes took that tragic journey, but the dingos had their own Trail of Tears. It's one of the saddest chapters in American history and a big part of yours because dingos were Native American dogs for many centuries."

He explained that the Trail of Tears happened under a famous American president named Andrew Jackson, who defeated the British at the Battle of New Orleans in the War of 1812. Jackson earned the nickname Old Hickory 'cause he was tough as nails. He had long felt that the Indians should be moved west of the Mississippi River where they would not pose a threat to white settlers.

"Build a fire under them," Jackson once said. "When it gets hot enough, they'll go."

Not long after Old Hickory got elected president, Congress passed a law forcing several tribes to move to Oklahoma, and nearly fifty thousand were forced to go there over the next ten years. According to Mr. Billy, one witness to the terrible suffering they had to undergo was a famous French author, Mr. Alexis de Tocqueville. He wrote in his book *Democracy in America* how he saw with his own eyes a band of Choctaws taken to the east bank of the Mississippi River near Memphis, where a boat was waitin' to take 'em across. The dogs had come with 'em, but just as they were about to board, the Army decided that the Choctaws had to leave their dogs behind. It was the dead of winter, and Mr. de Tocqueville saw huge masses of ice drifting in the water. The Indians were loaded onto a boat as their dogs watched on the bank. Then the famous author wrote—

"[N]ever will that solemn spectacle fade from my remembrance . . . As soon as these animals perceived that their masters were finally leaving the shore, they set up a dismal howl, and, plunging all together into the icy waters of the Mississippi, they swam after the boat."

Mr. Billy was sure that dismal howl was enough to melt even the coldest heart. What happened to the dogs? No one seems to know. But the way I figure, some of 'em musta drowned.

"Can you imagine what that was like, Honey?" Mr. Billy asked. "The dingos had always guarded Native American camps; their bond had always been unbreakable. Then suddenly it was destroyed in the worst way possible."

Somehow, I just knew that the dogs on the bank believed the companions they had always loved were leaving forever. They musta asked, *Where are they going? What will happen to us all?* They just *had* to follow. They could howl forever but they'd still be abandoned and alone . . . their sun and moon were vanishing. The campfires would never get lit again, and there'd be no soulmates to sit with them in the dark. The Great Spirit had deserted them, and no one knew why.

"No wonder they took the plunge into those icy waters," Mr. Billy told me.

More'n four thousand Cherokees would die on the way to Oklahoma, and many of us dingos barely survived on our Trail of Tears back to the swamps and lowlands of the southeast. Mr. Billy said we had no choice but to return to places we knew, and so we retreated to locations where food was easiest to find.

"You became wild dogs all over again but never lost your love for humans and never forgot the close companionship you once had with the Native Americans. The Great Spirit did not abandon you; it gave you the wonderful gift of being able to adapt and survive. That gift is what saved your tribe."

Miss Jane told me it was important never to forget just how close our relationship to the Native Americans was. She said experts who study ancient cultures had found dingo bones in clay pots buried thousands of years ago at entrances to Indian villages. It was a place of honor symbolizing how deeply they felt about us. They were sure our ties would last forever and in the afterlife too.

I could 'member Papa speakin' of the Great Vanishing when our closest companions, the Native Americans, had disappeared. I'd never thought any more about it, but the more Mr. Billy and Miss Jane talked, the more I knew I had something to live up to. One thing for sure. I was a whole lot more'n any stray, and way more'n any ditch dog.

The same day, somethin' terrible began to brew in the swamp, courtesy of Topper Guy. Turned out trappin' was way too slow for him, so he'd come up with a new way to get rid of the dingos. "It's top secret," he told Ragtop. "Deadly as dynamite. The best thing is I can make some money for clearin' the swamp of these varmints."

"Who's goin' to pay you?" Ragtop wanted to know.

"Keepin' that to myself." Topper Guy was cagey—real cagey— 'bout the whole thing.

Later on, Ragtop asked the Sidewinder (that's what Ace called Topper Guy), "What kind of varmints you aimin' to snag?"

"Coyotes, ditch dogs—you name it. Not a dime's worth of difference 'tween 'em."

"So, you'll just blow 'em all up? The hides sure won't be worth much then."

"Ain't sayin' I'm usin' real dynamite, but it'll work just the same—especially when I put my joy juice 'longside the Critter Trail."

"Sounds like you aim to stir up a Molotov cocktail."

"No, dumbass. This comes in a tiny dose and won't make a sound."

"Beats me what you're so dead-set to put out."

"Well, it's about the same as the juice in a stick of gum."

"Chiclets or Juicy Fruit?"

"Neither one, birdbrain. Just take my word for it. One sip's like a kick in the head from a mule."

It all turned out to be true. Topper Guy was goin' to spread a deadly poison all through the swamp. It would claim a whole lot of innocent lives.

Deadly poison spread along the Critter Trail by trappers kills two dingo pups.

PART TWO
Panic in the Swamp

9

The Phantom Arrives

The alarm bell first went off when a six-point buck turned up dead on the Critter Trail. Had a wild-eyed look but no fang marks on his carcass. That sent a shock wave through the swamp and a frantic search for answers. Had the killer killed for pure pleasure? Many said it had—that the able-bodied deer had up and died from fright. All agreed that the killer was big and mean and sure to strike again without warnin'.

Some paws pointed to an unidentified creature first seen on the cliff at Silver Bluff, high above the Savannah River, just before the deer turned up dead. A few had seen a brawny critter with a patchy coat of greyish brown runnin' through the trees. Several times, at a meetin' of the Swamp Elders, the intruder was called "the phantom." Some said its bite cut victims on the inside but left no mark on the outside. That caused panic in the swamp 'cause every critter knew it could be next.

Mr. Billy scoffed at what he called "phantom hysteria." More'n likely, he said, those who thought they'd seen a phantom had seen a big coyote instead. Turns out Mr. Billy knew all 'bout the coyote. He said it came from way, way off—a place called Glacier National Park, where the snow melt flows to the Arctic, Pacific, and Atlantic Oceans, a place where a critter needs a heavy coat to survive. Seems a Blackfoot Indian had seen the coyote six months earlier trackin' several kid goats through a grove of hemlocks and red cedars near a high mountain pass. A squall had come up just as he chased the kids through a patch of bear grass. The sure-footed goats had then scrambled onto glacial rocks where the coyote couldn't follow. After missin' out on the kill, he was seen the next mornin' on the valley floor sniffin' a breeze that carried the odor of coyote pee. He knew every coyote for miles, but the scent was not one he knew, so he tracked it to a patch of loose dirt and dead leaves 'longside a wildlife trail he often hunted. The coyote made a real bad mistake then by pawin' at the patch of leaves and dirt.

In a flash two steel jaws snapped tight around his foreleg. He yanked hard but had no chance to pull free—the trap was chained to a stake driven deep in the ground nearby. His struggles caused shootin' pains, so he finally settled down to wait. Late that day two trappers showed up—one carryin' a rifle, the other a catch pole with a noose on one end. The coyote jumped up and showed his fangs but quickly got collared by the noose. He howled in rage, lungin' at the pole and nearly knockin' the trapper off his feet.

Once he recovered, the trapper grinned and said, "Sure can put up a fight."

"A regular Geronimo," his partner joked.

"I thought Geronimo came from down south near the Mexican border—not here."

"I think that's right. But anyhow, you can see a side of him that's Apache fierce."

"Oh, and that's why you're namin' him Geronimo?"

"Well, why not?"

After that, the name stuck.

Once the trap was reset, a few drops of coyote urine were dribbled over it to lure another victim and scare off any coyote prey that might come near.

The trappers had been hired by a rancher who'd lost several lambs and felt sure a coyote had killed 'em. His first reaction was to shoot or poison any coyote on his ranch, to join the all-out

Geronimo—a lone sentinel at Silver Bluff high above the Savannah River.

war on coyotes taken up by many westerners as the only solution to their predator problems. Before he did that, the rancher had talked with a game warden who told him killin' off coyotes might backfire.

"You won't get 'em all," the game warden advised, "so only the fittest will survive. Their birthrates will go up and you'll get a new generation smarter than the one before. Coyotes get blamed for a lot they don't do. They don't chase down and eat the last rabbit. They feed instead on what's overpopulated and help balance nature that way."

The trappers had carried Geronimo off in a canvas bag. By midnight he was on a two-thousand-mile journey to a hunt pen hundreds of acres large near Bishopville, South Carolina. Soon after he got there, Mr. Billy and several friends showed up to train four Penn-Marydels, a dog breed fox hunters love for their musical voices and stamina. They'd come at dark in two trucks with two trained dogs in one, the untrained ones in the other.

After the two-hour ride, the hounds milled about in a dither, sniffin' and yappin'. Finally, one of the hunters held a sock doused with coyote urine to the older dog's noses. That revved two of the trained dogs, Rex and Tom Boy, up even more. When the sock got yanked away, the hunters started yellin' "go get 'em Rex . . . go get 'em Tom Boy."

The trained dogs bounded off through the brush with the untrained ones close behind. At first Rex and Tom Boy just sniffed with barely a yelp, but after a few minutes they found a few coyote tracks and started yelpin' as they tracked. As the scent grew stronger, they began to bawl in dead certainty.

They finally "jumped" Geronimo in a small grove of trees 'longside a creek where he'd bedded down for the night. The jump's that moment when the hounds first catch sight of a prey. Geronimo heard 'em comin' but waited lazily 'til they got close. He aimed to lead 'em on a merry chase. Soon as the hounds caught sight of him, he took off. By then the Penn-Marydels were howlin' to beat the band.

The hunters listened standin' in the glare of headlights. Cups were passed out and bourbon got poured.

"Hear that alto?" Mr. Billy exclaimed in high spirits. "That's Daisy; she's picking things up mighty fast."

"She'll learn stuff tonight she'll never forget," the man next to him replied.

Suddenly the woods went silent and the bawlin' stopped.

"Gone to ground," someone said. "That coyote's ducked 'em for good."

Geronimo had done just that: he'd led the Penn-Marydels on a lark for half an hour or more throughout the huge enclosure. When he finally got bored, he dodged into the hunt pen's escape area by squirmin' through a pipe that the Penn Marydels, who were twice his size, just couldn't get through. Inside the safety zone he could taunt the Penn-Marydels as much as he liked.

Mr. Billy told Miss Jane and me it seemed that Geronimo had lucked into a life of ease. He got fed every day and didn't have to hunt one bit. He could sleep all day and wouldn't get disturbed. The hunt pen owners even gave him shots and looked after his health. But Geronimo didn't want to be in a cage, and, even if the hunt pen was huge, that's exactly where he was.

His big break came that fall when a massive Cape Verde hurricane hit the state line between North and South Carolina. Several trees in the hunt pen fell on fences, so Geronimo just strolled out on an uprooted trunk. A few days later he was seen standin' on the chalk-white limestone cliff at Silver Bluff. There, high above the river, he appeared to be lord of all below. No wonder the critters thought of him as a phantom—one that scared victims to death and killed for pure pleasure.

Not long after my rescue, Ace found a lost dingo named Spear on the edge of Horse Creek and brought him back to Banbury Cross Farm. I went to see Spear right away to catch up on the news from the swamp, and I hoped to find out first and foremost if he'd seen anything of my pack. He said he hadn't but mentioned a trapper named Topper Guy had been diggin' holes 'longside the Critter Trail.

"He puts a plastic cup in each hole and pours somethin' inside," Spear told me. "I hear it's sweet to the taste, so I reckon he's puttin' out some kinda treat for the critters."

"Baloney!" I said. "That same Topper Guy came close to shootin' me. All he's after is hides. And besides that, he calls us ditch dogs—says he aims to wipe us out in the swamp once and for all."

"You sure of that?"

"Without a doubt. I was on the wrong end of his double-barreled shotgun. He'd have pulled the trigger if Miss Jane hadn't come along just in time."

"Sounds like you were mighty lucky and I'm glad you were. But I still wonder about the stuff he's puttin' in those cups. Once the critters taste how sweet it is they're bound to lap it up."

"I think you're right, but that stuff's bound to be dangerous. I wouldn't take even a tiny sip, and no one else should either."

"You may be right, but how you gonna stop him?"

"Don't know, but somehow I've gotta get word to my pack."

"Hope it ain't too late. No tellin' how many critters will drink that stuff and think it's great."

10

A Dingo Turns Up Dead

Papa always said once rumors start, they take on a life of their own. Soon after the dead deer was found, more critters started turnin' up dead—a possum, several rabbits, plus the skunk I was dumb enough to chase. (I'm sorry he croaked but it's hard to mourn a critter like that.) Strange to say they all bit the dust with the same wild-eyed look. That set off a new round of rumors that Geronimo had cast an evil spell on the swamp from the cliff at Silver Bluff.

By now I was frantic for any news of my pack. All I could do was sound out Spear who got little bits of news—mainly from strays that came to the kennel fence late at night. I learned no one had seen Mama, Papa, Sugar, or Popeye for days. Even worse, Spear doubted the latest rumors 'cause the dead critters all had dried foam on their mouths—just like the deer.

"Might not have been a spell," he said. "I'm thinkin' what's inside those cups 'longside the Critter Trail did 'em in."

It felt like I had a rattlesnake coiled up in the pit of my stomach.

"But look on the bright side," Spear added. "They say Geronimo's found a mate and won't have as much time for doin' in the critters."

Seems a romance had bloomed at Chimp's Corner, a beautiful spot named for the monkey-faced orchids that grow there.

Their faces look just like a chimp's and I usta go there to watch hummingbirds feedin' on orchid blooms. Spear said Geronimo spotted a female coyote there next to a clump of Spanish swords. She was shy but stood her ground when he went up to nuzzle her nose. Once they'd done their sniffin', she rose up, playfully, on her hind legs and put her paws on his shoulders. After that they frolicked 'til they wore slam out. Geronimo was hooked and seldom seen without her after that.

Not that they were seen much at all . . . which put the swamp on edge even more. Critters started seein' double . . . confusin' us with them . . . sayin' the phantoms were takin' over "out there." Dusk was the time of day that spooked 'em most, any movement in the shadows or hearin' the coyotes sing once the sun went down. That pair might've been cooin' love songs, but the swamp heard nothin' but the threat of doom.

That set me to thinkin' how hard it is to tell a coyote and a dingo apart. Our foxlike faces, tall pointy ears, and body build look a lot the same. A coyote's leaner, rangier, has a patchier coat, but we're still close cousins. We even build dens and birth pups the same. The den Geronimo built for his mate looked a lot like the one Papa built for us: a barrel-sized lean-to wedged under the clay-covered roots of a big pine uprooted in a storm . . . a roof of branches, twigs, and leaves mixed with clay. It was leak-proof just like ours.

Spear told me Geronimo called his mate Mamatoo 'cause she reminded him of his mama. Like other coyote pairs they were loyal to each other and never even made eyes at another coyote. Mamatoo got pregnant in early February and two months later had a litter of six pups. Once they opened their eyes, she took 'em out of the hole and put 'em in the sun where they looked like furry yellow balls. They rolled and tumbled, scratched and bit like brothers and sisters so often do.

Later that spring Geronimo and Mamatoo began teachin' the pups the foxlike pounce coyotes and dingos use to catch lizards, frogs, and other small fry. They also learned to speak coyote: yips, yelps, and barks the pack would use to track game and stay in touch with one another. That's one place where we differ: a dingo talks mostly with its fishhook tail, 'specially when out on a hunt.

Once the pups had learned the basics, Geronimo and Mamatoo took 'em on their first hunt. It started in a small clearin' where the pups were hidden in a clump of tall grass near the middle with Geronimo on one side, Mamatoo the other. They'd just started barkin' back and forth when two shots were fired at Mamatoo. Splinters flew on the pine bark just above her head. She ducked and gave a frantic "come quick" call to her pups.

By then Geronimo had spotted the shooter and could see he was fixin' to shoot again. He looked back across the clearin' but by that point Mamatoo had vanished, so he thought she was down. With no thought at all for his own safety, he bounded into the center of the clearin' to find his mate . . . and three shots whizzed overhead. But a welcome sight had greeted him once he crossed the clearin'. Mamatoo had the pups in tow, leadin' them, quick as she could, back to the den, where they all got inside.

Once inside the den, she warned the pups not to make a sound . . . to hunker down to wait 'til the danger passed. Geronimo finally went out for a look-see and saw a man sittin' on a stump at the edge of the clearin' havin' a smoke. He had a stringy beard and a gun shell vest. When Mamatoo heard he was still there she said they'd all hafta stay put 'til noon the next day.

When Spear told me all this, we started talkin' 'bout what makes it so hard to tell the difference 'tween a dingo and a coyote.

"For one thing you've got to know what to look for," he said.

"We may be close cousins," I replied, "but there's still one mighty big difference."

"I don't think so."

"Yes, there is. A coyote's got no room in the heart for humans . . . the dingo does."

The next day I heard Ace say a dingo had turned up dead in the swamp not far from Silver Bluff.

Topper Guy had taken the carcass to Scooter's Bar and Eats to show off like some trophy.

"I found this coyote alongside the wildlife trail in the swamp," he crowed.

Someone in the crowd scoffed, "Better start lookin' before you shoot. That ain't a coyote, you got a ditch dog."

Topper Guy shrugged and said, "Ain't a dime's worth of difference 'tween a ditch dog and a coyote, but I didn't shoot her anyhow."

"Then how'd you bag her?" another patron asked.

"Ain't sayin' but my work's all comin' together. You might say some of 'em just gave up the ghost."

The Sidewinder was actin' cagier than ever. He didn't want folks knowin' what he was really up to.

I was with Ace when he told Miss Jane about the dead dingo at Scooter's. She gave Ace the steely-eyed look only an alpha mom can give.

"That poor dingo," Miss Jane said. "Her mama will feel somehow she failed her."

I shook all over when she said that. A terrible thought had come to me: *What if that dead dingo is Mama?* I wanted to know she and the pack were safe more'n anything in the whole world.

11

Trip to Town

The very next mornin' Miss Jane told Ace she aimed to do whatever it took to stamp out the new and dangerous threat to dingos. The three of us then drove into Aiken to get some posters printed up. She paid extra for a rush order, and the printer promised to have 'em ready by noon.

"While we wait, I'd like to show you a bit of the town," she told me.

As a swamp dog, I'd never been to town before—any town, let alone one as pretty as Aiken. She told me the place had just been named one of "America's Most Distinctive Destinations" by some big magazine. It was easy to see why: live oaks with long beards of Spanish moss had grown over many of its streets. Everywhere I looked I saw grand homes, beautiful parks, and large green spaces.

Miss Jane made a quick stop at the Wilcox Hotel where famous politicians, big shots in business, and even kings and queens liked to stay. While she was inside Ace said, "The blue-noses hang out here. You'll see—this little town's packed full of rich folks. Miss Jane and Mr. Billy ain't hurtin', but they don't put on airs. They hang with high muckety-mucks and plain folks too. I'd say they're smooth with just about anybody but the likes of that sorry whatshisname . . .?"

I thumped my tail hard three times.

Ace laughed. "I know what you're sayin': whatshisname has gotta be Topper Guy."

Ace told me not to worry, that Topper Guy was no match for Miss Jane. He then told how she'd saved a small dingo pup from a white owl that snatched it just outside a birthin' hole dug by its mama.

"That owl looked like a jumbo jet rumblin' down the runway tryin' to get off the ground," Ace told me with a laugh. "Miss Jane was workin' in a flower bed and just happened to see the owl swoop down to snatch the pup in its talons. She grabbed a rake and took off after that thief and whacked him good just in the nick of time. The owl dropped the pup and soared off. It was a mighty lucky pup," I'd say. After hearin' that, it seemed to me that Ace might be right: that the Sidewinder would have a hard time getting the best of Miss Jane.

As we rode 'round Aiken, I 'specially liked the color of the town. It almost made me feel I was at home in the swamp after a hard rain. The place was gourd green, as Papa would say. Some of its mansions had ivy-covered walls. One called the Green Boundary Club had been turned into a supper club where members of the town's famous Winter Colony dined and played backgammon, bridge, and croquet. Miss Jane told me people "dressed to the nines" for Green Boundary Christmas balls. "That means tucked up and mighty fancy," Ace 'splained.

"I'll have you invited to this year's ball," Miss Jane promised. When I gave her a worried look, she laughed. "I suppose you don't have a thing to wear. Don't fret . . . we'll find something perfect for the season—a red collar, perhaps, with green holly leaves." I wanted to ask what good's a collar in the cold. I'd rather have a warm sweater anytime. Then again, Miss Jane knows what a well-dressed dingo ought to wear.

Later, we took a short walk in Hitchcock Woods, the greenest place of all. "You're lookin' at one of the last great stands of longleaf pine left anywhere," Ace told me. "See how thick their trunks are? When lightning strikes and sets off a hot fire they still survive. The fire burns off the pine needles and wire grass on the forest floor . . . turns it to ash as rich as fertilizer. That way seeds from these big trees sprout fast."

I learned that the town got its start when the railroad connected Charleston to a barge port not too far from Silver Bluff. Cotton loaded in Aiken got shipped to the coast and on to mills in England. It was the world's longest railroad when it opened in 1830—136 miles, no less. Times were good then for cotton but turned bad with the Civil War. The town suffered terrible losses—a quarter of those sent off got killed or injured—but held out to a bitter end. The Battle of Aiken turned out to be the last Confederate victory.

"Folks around here are still proud of whippin' General Sherman after his famous March to the Sea," Ace said. "'Course I don't hold with that one bit. All that battle did was put off when black folks got their freedom." Seemed to me that Ace had a point. He always spoke his mind . . . let the chips fall where they may, even on toes if need be.

Once we got the posters from the printer, Ace held one up for me to see. It had a picture of a dingo that looked like Papa. Ace then read: Attention All Hunters—Illegal to Kill a Dingo Dog. These dogs are gentle and love humans . . . It went on to explain the differences between a dingo and a coyote . . . also urged hunters not to shoot a coyote unless it was a threat to pets or livestock.

After that we drove around town puttin' posters on lamp posts, telephone poles, and even the sides of buildings. On the way back home, we heard a news flash on the radio 'bout several pets in Aiken gettin' killed. Seemed a half dozen or more cats and small dogs had been attacked 'round town. Their owners had been shocked to find half-eaten carcasses.

Miss Jane and Ace put up posters saying it is illegal to shoot dogs like me.

"Who caused these chilling deaths remains unclear," the announcer said. "But wildlife experts say coyotes have invaded our area and are probably responsible. Stray dogs also may have done in the pets. Animal control has issued a warning to all pet owners: Do not—repeat, do *not*—allow your dog to run off leash. And do not let your cat out of sight at any time."

Over the summer Aiken had been hit with one of the worst droughts ever, causin' sharply lower food supplies. Even the number of voles, insects, and frogs was down, which meant that dingos and coyotes had less to eat. In the swamp the battle for survival was a daily struggle, but now it had entered a new, more dangerous stage. If the coyotes were eatin' Aiken's pets, they could be doin' somethin' just as bad in the swamp. Defenseless dingo pups there would make 'em a mighty tasty meal.

12

Trigger-Happy Hunters

Once word of the pet killin's spread, the swamp wasn't the only place in a panic—the town was in one too. Folks got all riled up over who'd done it. Most blamed coyotes but some said it was bobcats or stray dogs. One upset caller told a radio station he'd seen a panther in his garden at dusk. A game warden came on to assure that panthers weren't native to the uplands and had never been sighted there before. The newspaper hotline was overrun with ideas on what to do, includin' one to set up a seal bopper brigade to patrol neighborhoods where pets got killed.

The night after the news broke, Scooter's Bar was packed to the gills and just a-buzzin' with theories 'bout how the pets were gettin' killed. The bar was a known hangout for hunters and trappers, so pet-owning victims had even come to offer rewards for revenge.

Ace called Scooter's "a down-on-your-luck saloon, a home away from home for beer-drinkin' guys who don't pay enough attention to their wives. Never been in there, but I've got my sources." He said the crowd all knew the burly barkeep whose beard looked a lot like the pirate Blackbeard's. He drew pitchers of draft behind the horseshoe bar while a waitress in a tight football jersey carried trays of beer 'round the room. "The guys all wanted her attention," Ace said, "but she wasted no time on small talk."

A moose head behind the bar had an ammo belt hangin' from one antler. A sign on the wall said: PACKING HEAT? DRINK AND DRAW! Those words came from the barrel of a smokin' gun. The South Carolina Revolutionary War flag, with its quarter moon above a palmetto tree, decorated one wall with Christmas lights that blinked year-round.

A few beagles and coon hounds lounged on the floor waitin' for a tidbit to get tossed their way. They were undisturbed by the customer catcalls, blarin' TVs, and a Cosmic Blast jukebox playin' country and western songs.

All eyes turned toward the front door 'bout 6 p.m. when a TV cameraman, a sound man with a long boom mike, and a reporter named Sarah pushed their way inside. The barkeep said "Have at it" when she asked for permission to interview a few customers. Pointin' to a hulkin' fellow in a John Deere hat, he advised, "There's your man. Nothin' left of his cat 'cept the tail."

The aggrieved one was leanin' against the pool table when Sarah approached and asked for his name.

"Rucker, Wilbur Ray Rucker. My wife's cried her eyes out over this. Little Lottie was our pride and joy and wouldn't harm a flea."

"When did you find her?"

"Yesterday just 'fore dark."

"Any idea what happened?"

"Pretty sure some ditch dog did it. I came here to put up a reward. I'm hopin' somebody will give these sorry rascals just what they deserve."

"What sort of reward?"

"Cash on the barrel . . . five hundred bucks to the man who takes out the killers."

"And what do you mean by takes out?"

"Trap 'em, shoot 'em—do whatever it takes to stop these low-down curs."

"Yes sir, and I'm just the man for the job." These words came from just beyond Wilbur Ray Rucker's shoulder. Then the mike shifted to a man with a scruffy beard and a well-worn ammo vest.

"Would you identify yourself for our viewers?"

"Name's Topper Guy Sawyer. I trap in these parts. This here's my partner—Ragtop." He elbowed a sleepy-lookin' guy with a rebel flag bandanna 'round his noggin.

"Would you give us your take on this, Mr. Sawyer?"

"We're all agreed that Mr. Rucker's got cause to be madder'n hell. For certain, his cat was killed by a vicious beast. The kind that would do this . . . well, some call 'em swamp dogs and some call 'em coyotes. I can say, based on my long experience, that there ain't a dime's worth of difference 'tween 'em. A whole bunch of these critters live back in the swamp not far from where I live near the mouth of Timm's Creek."

"So, you've actually seen them?"

"Every day near 'bout. They're wild and mean. Little cats and dogs don't stand a chance wherever one of these devils crops up. The little ones are just a tasty morsel—that's all."

"But the game warden has blamed coyotes for these killings," Sarah pressed. "He says the lack of food has forced them to be much more aggressive."

"Maybe he's right and maybe he's wrong. I brought one outta the swamp just the other day. It turned out to be a coyote, which is just the same as a ditch dog."

"Do you plan to pursue the reward Mr. Rucker is offering?"

"Damn straight I do. I'll be headin' into the swamp first thing tomorrow."

"Me too," Ragtop chimed in. "We'll be loaded for bear . . . I mean ditch dogs."

On the 11 p.m. news that night, Sarah reported that several hunters would head to the swamp at daybreak to avenge the dead pets. She said the hunters were targeting coyotes or ditch dogs.

Topper Guy calls us "ditch dogs" on TV.

Miss Jane and Mr. Billy were about to turn in for the night when they saw Sarah's report on the news. "This is awful—those poor dogs," she exclaimed. "We've got to do something."

Mr. Billy switched off the TV. "Guess I'll get up at five and drive out to Timm's Creek. Maybe I can head them off. But from the sound of it I'm not too optimistic. Sounds like those hunters will shoot at any dingo they see."

"We know very well that a dingo would *never* do such a thing. They're gentle, loving creatures."

"I know," Mr. Billy glumly replied. "But when a mob gets whipped up, it has no interest in the truth. These characters intend to make the dingos pay no matter what."

When I heard that conversation, I told myself Geronimo had cast an evil spell on the swamp. Somehow, he'd shifted the blame to hang it right around our necks.

13

I'm Gonna Be a Star

Never did figure out who left the gate open and let all twelve of Miss Jane's Canadian geese stroll outta the pen and waddle down to the pond where they, too, could get caught by a coyote. If that happened, the clipped-wing honkers wouldn't stand a chance. They couldn't fly off a haystack in a flag-rippin' breeze.

Ace and me had just come out of the Clipper when we saw the honkers closin' in on the pond. If they ever got in the water, we'd never get 'em back to the pen.

As I bounded off toward the pond, Ace yelled "Go Honey go!"

They were near 'bout to the edge of the water when I cut 'em off. As I ran along the bank I barked as loud as I could. That stopped 'em dead in their tracks. For a moment they just craned their necks in surprise—figurin', I s'pose, on whether to do an end run. Their white chinstraps were stretched tight when the biggest, a male (Ace called him a drake), came hissin' at me to beat the band. As mad as he was, I still held my ground and let loose with more loud barks. He stopped just short of my shadow but kept on hissin'.

That's when Ace ran up waving his arms and shoutin' "shoo, shoo, shoo." Much to our surprise the honkers, includin' the drake, turned and waddled back up the hill, though a few did straggle off to the side.

"Herd, Honey, herd!" Ace ordered.

Wasn't too sure what that meant, but my instincts told me to chase 'em toward the center of the lawn. Then, dashin' and dodgin' fast as I could, I got the stragglers formed up in a flock and soon had 'em movin' up the hill and back toward the pen. Ace threw the gate open wide and stood aside as the geese waddled in. Soon as they did, he slammed the gate and latched it.

"Great work, Honey! Had no idea you could do that."

His praise made me feel mighty proud. My first time herdin' and it was fun—'specially chasin' down the stragglers.

"You're jitterbug-quick, girl," Ace said with a flush. "I'm impressed with your reactions and how fast you can fly." He knelt down, patted my head, and gave my back a warm rub . . . even let me lick his face, which he rarely let me do.

"I can see a whole new world for you to conquer. No tellin' what you could do in an agility contest."

Later that day I heard him tell Miss Jane: "You shoulda seen Honey herdin' those runaway geese. Never seen anything like it. That dog's quick as a water bug and can turn on a dime. If she's trained right, she could be a real champion."

They talked for a bit in a hush-hush way until Miss Jane finally said, "Well, why don't we give agility a try?" But then she had a second thought: "Before Honey starts agility drills, she's got to master Canine Good Citizenship. She needs to learn the basics of sit, stay, and come before anything else."

"Makes sense to me," Ace replied.

That afternoon Ace took me to the wide patch of lawn between the Big House and the pond. "Okay, Honey, let's work on your manners." What he didn't tell me was how hard it would be. I was full of energy and ran circles 'round Ace as we approached the pond. Suddenly he stopped and said, "We'll work first on the sit command. I want you to *sit* now." I had no idea what he meant and gave him a dumb look. Ace patiently held a small slice of hot dog ("treat," he called it) just above my nose. I wanted that morsel in the worst way, so I kept raisin' my nose 'til my hiney touched the ground. When it did, Ace said loudly, "Good job Honey!" and dropped the tasty morsel in my mouth. I gobbled it down and he told me to sit again. I gave him another dumb look, hopin' for a treat. "No drooling," Ace sternly advised and then gave my backside a firm downward push. "Sit!" he ordered once more. I did as I was told and got another hot dog slice. "Good job!" he said. We did this over and over 'til I finally learned that *sit* meant to put my bottom on the ground . . . and that I'd get a treat every time I did.

Over the next few days Ace and I worked on the down-stay command, the come command, and how to walk on a leash without pullin' and jerkin'. It was hard, but I also learned to pass another dog and not lunge . . . and not to sniff too much either. I liked listenin' to and followin' Ace's commands. I loved to please and felt like part of his team.

"We're buildin' a bond, girl," Ace would say. "Like stone buddies, as we say down south." Hearin' him say that made me want to please him even more.

Not too long after Ace started me on Canine Good Citizenship, he told Miss Jane: "Honey's become a model citizen. She's got all the commands down pat. You can have her dine with the black-tie set and she won't beg for a single crumb."

"You're sure about that?"

"Certain as how she got those geese penned." He pointed to the honkers I'd rounded up after their jail-break.

Miss Jane replied, "I suppose that means we're ready for Stage Two."

"Agility training," Ace said with a pearly smile.

"Let's do it."

"Mighty big jumpin' beans!" he exclaimed. "Goin' straight to the top, ain't we, Honey?"

"Aren't we," Miss Jane corrected.

"Aren't we, Honey?"

Their enthusiasm excited me. I cut loose with a few high-pitched barks to let 'em know how ready I was. From the way they talked, my hunch was agility would be easy as fallin' off a log.

But agility was way harder than Canine Good Citizenship. I doubted at first that I could even do it. I'd have to walk on a teeter-totter, run up and down the A-frame, jump through a tire, run tunnels, and clear jumps higher than I was. Toughest of all was workin' my way through the weave poles. All these obstacles were really hard . . . took a long time to get the hang of it. Even when I did, we still had to work on timing. I'd have to run the entire obstacle course in no more than thirty-five seconds—lickety-split, to say the least.

One Saturday Ace took me to Flea-flickers, a covered arena with a full obstacle course. He liked how I ran so much he convinced Miss Jane to buy a weave pole, a tunnel, and a teeter-totter so we could practice on the lawn.

"Once Honey masters these obstacles," he told Miss Jane, "she'll be competitive anywhere she runs. She just might win the whole she-bang."

By then, I was bustin' out all over with confidence. No wonder! Ace kept tellin' me, "Girl, you're gonna be a star." Wasn't too sure what that meant but I knew we were aimin' high.

As my times improved, he'd say, "We're almost ready for the Big Time." Once we were, that meant we'd head up to Teamworks Dog Trainers, which had just opened a state-of-the art agility arena north of Raleigh.

I couldn't wait to get there—to find out if I was really and truly gonna be a star.

Just then a grim sight knocked me for a loop. One of the farm's tractor drivers came back from a rabbit hunt near Silver Bluff with two dead dingo pups. He'd found 'em at Chimp's Corner curled up just short of a stump hole full of water.

"Looked to me like they were desperate for somethin' to drink," he told Ace.

"Wonder why?"

"No tellin' but you can see they're both healthy . . . not more'n three months old, I'd say.

"Any fang marks on 'em?"

"Not that I could tell, but take a look."

Ace went over the small furry bodies with his hands. "We can rule out coyotes, that's for sure."

"So, what's that leave?"

"I just don't know," Ace replied, "but I'm takin' these little critters to the Game Department. Maybe they can figure out the cause of death in their lab."

"A good idea. Maybe they can test why these little buggers wanted something to drink so bad."

14

Timm's Creek Massacre

By sunrise, the hunters were at the boat ramp 'cross from Silver Bluff on a wild stretch of the Savannah River. Later on, we got the full story when Ragtop spilled his guts.

From what he said, Topper Guy was braggin' from the git-go how he'd bag his limit 'fore dark. His buddies, Bobby Ray and Smiley, had hauled their boat to the launch behind a battered blue Ford 150 pickup. After Bobby Ray backed it down the ramp, Smiley untied the bow strap and climbed aboard. He lowered the outboard engine into the water, then backed off and out into the stream. After Bobby Ray parked the rig, Smiley picked him up at the dock. Topper Guy and Ragtop blew cigarette smoke from a second boat while watchin' the launch. They'd motored over at the crack of dawn from the shack where my hide was saved by Miss Jane. Both boats were flat bottomed, drew very little water, and could go deep into the swamp.

"Just follow us," Topper Guy yelled to Bobby Ray and Smiley as he nosed into midstream. "I'm buyin' beer for anybody who can outgun me and that includes my hair-brained partner." He followed that with a rowdy laugh which Ragtop said he didn't 'preciate at all.

The boats cruised past Silver Bluff and slowed at the entrance to Timm's Creek, which narrowed to canal size once they passed Topper Guy's place. In a few spots, the props had to be raised to get past mud banks and shoals. As the boats approached the heart of the swamp, the stream narrowed to the point that the hunters could touch the marsh grass on either side with a paddle. By then water depth measured only eighteen inches or so.

"Seen any gators here?" Smiley yelled to Topper Guy.

"You bet—plenty. Keep a eye out for mud slides; that's where they crawl in and out of the water." A few moments later the party passed a mud slide—a mucky opening not three feet wide through the marsh.

A bit later the boats reached a wide expanse of green lily pads and wax myrtles, a small tree that thrives in marshes. The hunters had reached the heart of the bald cypress swamp and their boats were scrapin' bottom. At that point they got out and pulled the boats through the lily pads to a shoreline of oozy muck. It was a place few humans ever set foot on. But critters abounded: white-tailed deer, mink, raccoons, woodpeckers, herons, turtles, snakes, and many others, includin' dingos, who've lived there since the Native Americans left.

Once the hunters reached dry ground, Topper Guy retrieved a small gadget from his backpack to show the others: "See this amazin' little gizmo? A real magnet . . . gives out a distressed rabbit call or cries like a pup. Put it on the ground in a clearin' and let it wiggle. Curiosity always draws the critters to it."

Next Topper Guy gave each of his buddies a box of gun shells. "Scattershot," he said, holdin' up a shell. "Special made for coyotes so they're perfect for ditch dogs, too. Got pellets somewhat bigger'n BBs." All four hunters carried 12-gauge shotguns for shootin' at close range . . . targets of thirty to fifty yards.

"All right, let's fan out," Topper Guy ordered. "We'll each be hunting quarter-mile sections around these boats. Stay on the east-west or north-south lines of the compass. Ragtop and I'll take the east, the rest of you spread out on the other sections. Tote what you shoot back to the boats and we'll haul it out to

Scooter's." As they left, he reminded the others that their prey would be very shy. "If you move even a little, they're bound to see you," he warned.

A short time later he stationed Ragtop in a small clearing full of ferns, decaying logs, and rhododendrons. When they turned on the distressed rabbit call, Ragtop groused, "That thing's spooky and I ain't happy stayin' here alone. If a wild boar comes along, this pea shooter (he grabbed the barrel of his shotgun) wouldn't even slow him down."

"Pay attention knucklehead. I'm aimin' to collect that reward. Welch on me and you'll wish a boar had come along 'fore I could get my hands on you."

"Listen—I don't 'preciate the threat. I can hold up my end any day."

With that, Topper Guy moved on to his zone, the last quarter-mile section. He set up in a milkweed patch near several bald cypresses after spottin' several vole burrows and croakin' frogs. With food close by, he figured coyote or ditch dog dens would be too.

He was ready to turn on the rabbit sound when two quick *bang-bangs* broke the early mornin' silence. They came from close by, so he figured Ragtop had shot one, maybe two of their prey. A few minutes later two more shots were fired from farther off. Bobby Ray or Smiley musta got one, Topper Guy told himself.

The rabbit's distress call soon got on his nerves. Sounded like a baby bawlin' from a bad case of colic. No wonder it spooked Ragtop. He switched on the puppy cry but soon decided it was just as hard to listen to.

Hunkerin' down at the base of a tree, he waited and scanned the cypress grove, certain that his prey would come from that direction. Suddenly he sensed movement—nothin' he could see, just a feelin' of somethin' in the shadowy trees. His prey must have heard the puppy cry and was comin' to nose it out.

Then he saw a ginger-colored stray stalk in stealth from the trees. Lean and taut frame with tall pointy ears, it slinked forward in a crouch.

"Come on . . . come on . . . just a little closer," Topper Guy muttered over his gun sight. "Now turn to the side. Give me a heart shot."

The dingo kept creepin' forward cautiously, as if it sensed danger. It was roughly forty yards off when . . .

POW!

The dingo slumped to the ground. Its ears twitched for a moment, then went limp.

"Heart shot!" Topper Guy yelled in triumph. "Right through the ticker."

As the afternoon wore on, shots rang out over and over as the blood bath continued. The rabbit and puppy calls had worked, and dingo curiosity had done 'em in.

About half an hour before calling it quits, Topper Guy switched off the sound gadget so he could try another trick. He fetched a turkey feather from his backpack and tied a fishing line on the quill end. He then tied the fishin' line to a tree limb and watched the feather dance on the light breeze.

"I want to see how much curiosity these rascals really have," he said knowingly. "This thing oughta work like a charm."

He then hid in the bushes to wait. 'Fore long a dingo had crept close enough to the dancin' feather to get shot. This one, however, was a nursin' mother. "Got to be a litter of pups close by somewhere," Topper Guy muttered. "But ain't wastin' no time on 'em."

Late that afternoon the hunters put their trophies on display in the Scooter's parking lot. Topper Guy announced he'd shot the most—five of the twelve taken.

"Means I win the money. How we stand on that Brother Rucker?"

"Wilbur Ray stepped out from the crowd. "You're a man of your word Topper Guy. My wife and I 'preciate what you've done and are happy to pony up. Thanks for standin' up for our little Lottie."

"Beer's on me," Topper Guy shouted to the crowd once he got the cash.

He then stuck a muddy boot under the hind leg of one of the dead dogs and flipped it over. "See how I nailed this 'un with a heart shot. A pretty good one too 'cause I was a long way out when I pulled the trigger."

"Don't git much better than that," Ragtop enthused.

The next morning Miss Jane and Mr. Billy were horrified to see photos of the dead dogs on the front page of the *Aiken Standard*. One showed Topper Guy flippin' one over with a muddy boot. Mr. Billy had driven out to Topper Guy's place early the previous morning to try to head the whole thing off, but the hunters were gone by the time he got there. As she stared at the photo, Miss Jane shed no tears. She had a steely-eyed look instead.

"I'm going to that roadhouse tomorrow to talk to those rascals," she vowed. "This is an absolute disgrace—shooting innocent, loving dogs. Someone's got to put a stop to this once and for all."

My heart sank when I heard 'em talkin'. Members of my own pack could be among the victims. I shuddered to think of them layin' in that parkin' lot and gettin' flipped over by a muddy boot. The dingos hadn't killed the first pet—I was sure of that. So why would anyone want to shoot one of us?

Suddenly, I realized how much I missed my pack: the nuzzles I'd get from Mama's nose, playin' with Popeye and Sugar, seein' Papa patch the roof of our den. Sure, I'd found a great home: Miss Jane, Mr. Billy, and Ace had been so kind, so good to me, I really couldn't ask for more. But I was homesick just the same.

I missed our cozy little den——how on the coldest days we curled up together in one big ball of fur. And I couldn't bear to think that those I loved most were bein' shot at and maybe killed. Worst of all, there was nothin' I could do 'cept hope the shots missed. And that was no help at all. It just left me feelin' blue——like somebody had shut down the Critter Trail for good.

PART THREE
One for All, All for One

15

High-Stakes Bet

I was scared stiff when Miss Jane told me she was goin' to Scooter's to confront Topper Guy and aimed to take me along. Just as we were leavin', the phone rang. I could tell she'd be a while, so I sneaked in the den and hid behind the sofa. Okay, so I did hear her call once she put the phone down, but I wasn't 'bout to come out. Much as I loved Miss Jane, I couldn't take a chance on what the Sidewinder would do if he got half a chance.

Then I heard her callin' as she came into the den, "Honey, I know you're in here somewhere. I've got to have your help. It's up to us to save the dingos in the swamp."

That was almost enough to bring me out, but somehow it felt like I was glued to the spot.

"Please don't worry," she said. "I promise not to let Topper Guy hurt you."

I had no idea what she wanted me to do, but I couldn't resist the warmth in her voice. I peeked out from behind the sofa.

"There you are!" she exclaimed and gathered me up in her arms. We went straight to her big black truck and she plopped me on the front seat. I was still nervous—pantin' with my tongue hanging out, so she lowered my window halfway. "Okay, now you can stick your head out. That always seems to help you relax."

We headed then to Scooter's where Topper Guy and his buddies drank beer late in the day. "Miss Jane looked like a million," as Ace would say, behind the wheel. She wore a white lace blouse, a navy blue blazer, and tan slacks. Not a hair out of place, chin up, tight-lipped, and dead serious for sure. Even so, I sensed that she was nervous, 'cause her eyes blinked a lot faster than normal.

As we parked, she spied Topper Guy's truck. "Don't worry, I won't go inside and leave you all alone." Instead, she politely asked two guys smokin' at the door if they'd go in and find Topper Guy. In no time at all, the Sidewinder came out with Ragtop on his heels. I watched that pair close from where I sat behind the steerin' wheel.

When he saw Miss Jane, Topper Guy said, "Well, look who's here Ragtop—the lady we snookered on that ditch dog. Did you come for another mutt? Tell me what I can do for you ma'am."

"I'd like to have a frank conversation on a subject of mutual interest," Miss Jane replied. She was standin' in front of the truck when the pair walked up.

"Can't imagine what that might be," Topper Guy came back in a surly way.

"The senseless killing of innocent dogs," she bluntly replied.

"Now hold on here. You know, good as I do, these ditch dogs have been on a killin' spree. Everybody in Aiken knows they're killin' pets right and left. Somebody had to stop 'em; all we done was our duty. You might call it a public service."

"I understand that you may *think* what you did is right, but I can assure you this is a case of mistaken identity."

"Say what?"

"The ditch dogs you keep referring to are an ancient breed—most likely the oldest in North America; they're called the American Dingos, or Carolina Dogs. I breed them on my farm because they're becoming extinct. I can assure you that not one of these dogs has a mean bone in its body."

"Well, you're welcome to your opinion. None of us here sees it that way."

"I can assure you, sir, that what I have to say is *not* mere opinion; it's based on scientific and historical research, as well as my own practical experience in raising these dogs for the past eighteen years."

"You sure got a lot of highfalutin' ideas, but I'm the only one here that knows what goes on in the swamp."

"And what might that be?"

"These dogs'll kill anythin' that gits in their way."

"Can you cite evidence to support that?"

"Just what I seen with my own eyes."

"With all due respect, I have to take exception. These dogs were the camp dogs of the Native Americans. They're intensely loyal, and they make wonderful pets. There's nothing vicious about them at all. Just take a look at the innocent face behind my steering wheel; you can easily confirm what I'm saying."

"That the ditch dog you bought off'n me?"

She nodded yes.

"She's mighty lucky Topper Guy didn't put 'er down just 'fore you drove up," Ragtop put in.

"What you planned to do with her is beside the point now. Her life—the life of any American Dingo—shouldn't depend on luck. I'm telling you the breed is faced with extinction now that the coyotes have come into our part of the country. People simply can't tell them apart. And I can assure you that the small pets were killed by coyotes and not dingos."

"Hate to tell you, but that dog you bought ain't good for nothin'."

"With all due respect, Mr. Sawyer, you're dead wrong. That dog—her name is Honey—is going to be a champion."

"Champion of what—pet killin'?"

I could tell Miss Jane was close to blowin' her stack, but she calmly replied, "No, she's going to be a champion of agility. Agility happens to be the most popular—and demanding—dog sport in the world."

"Well, I wouldn't bet a single marble on her."

"Then perhaps you'd like to bet against her winning a major agility championship."

"Come to think of it, I just might do that."

"A championship happens to be coming up at a famous place called Purina Farms outside St. Louis, where top-notch dog agility contests are held. They will be hosting an event called Sportsman exactly one month from now. Honey's already entered."

"You gotta be kiddin'—that dog will end up chasin' its tail." That comment drew a couple of approving snorts from the Sidewinder's sidekick.

"That's where we disagree," Miss Jane insisted. "And so, I'd like to settle this with a no-nonsense wager. Are you open to such a wager Mr. Sawyer?"

"I just might be. Watcha got in mind?"

"I propose to wager my finest stud horse, Maestro Magic, against your promise not to hunt another dingo dog again. In order to make good on that, you would need to wager the hardware displayed in the back window of your truck."

Topper Guy shot a glance at his truck.

"She aims to take away that gun," Ragtop advised.

"I got that, dumbass." Turning back toward Miss Jane, he asked, "What's a horse like your Maestro Magic worth?"

"You're welcome to get an appraisal, but I'd say a minimum of five thousand dollars."

"Better jump on that," Ragtop enthused.

"Dammit, I told you to keep your trap shut." Topper Guy thought for a minute and then said, "Lady, you got yourself a deal."

Miss Jane held out her hand and the two shook, but I was sure she'd wash hers first chance she got.

On the drive back to the farm it dawned on me just how much would be ridin' on how I did. I'd never been to an agility championship—let alone run in one. But Miss Jane would be dependin' on me, and I didn't even want to think about the smirk on Topper Guy's face if I fell flat on my hiney. Knowing that the fate of the dingo tribe in the swamp depended on how I ran made the bet even scarier.

I musta been shakin' 'cause Miss Jane told me, "Just relax, Honey. Like Ace said, you're gonna be a star. We all have complete confidence in you."

I was glad they felt that way and hoped their confidence would rub off on me. I wondered how I got into such a tight spot. It felt like I'd been caught in a trap, and would have to gnaw my leg off to get it out.

16

Practice Makes Perfect

Our visit to Scooter's made it very clear that Miss Jane wouldn't leave *anything at all* to chance. She meant for me to be in tip-top shape and fully prepared when we went west to the big agility championship in late September. So, soon as we got back from meetin' with the Sidewinder, she sat down with Ace and told him all about the bet. They decided on a plan for honin' my skills on every obstacle I'd face at the Sportsman's agility championship.

Three days after that a van arrived at the farm, backed up to the edge of the lawn, and unloaded another weave pole, a second tunnel, a new A-frame, a tire jump, a wall jump, and several bar jumps. With the stuff we already had, it made for a complete obstacle course like I'd have to run at Sportsman's.

"Okay, Honey," Ace said, "now we can get down to serious business. You'll learn to take every obstacle in the right order and then work on time. To win you'll have to make a fault-free run. Once you do that, it all comes down to time: the dog with the fastest time wins the grand championship. Got that straight?"

Wasn't sure 'cause that was a whole lot to take in. The weave pole had been the toughest by far. Wormin' my way in and out 'tween six poles seemed to stump me every time. And now I had a second set of poles to get through. Just thinkin' 'bout that made me pant. How in the world would I ever do it? I had just got the hang of the teeter-totter and the tunnel, and here they were pushin' me to master all these new obstacles. To run 'em without a single fault was more'n I could imagine. I got jumpy and nervous over how easy it was to screw up. Then, to top it all off, Ace told me I'd have to run the whole course in thirty-five seconds or less to win.

"Don't want to overload your circuits Honey, but we'd better go full bore. I didn't know what he meant by circuits, but Ace was full of strange expressions—like *throwin' so and so a curve.* Somehow, I knew that was what he was was throwin' me now.

There was only one way out of this mess: practice, practice, and more practice. Actually, I liked that because once I started runnin' the obstacle course I forgot everything else—all about Sportsman's, the Sidewinder, wagers involvin' guns, and Maestro Magic—you name it. One thing for sure: I would do anything I could to keep from lettin' Miss Jane and Ace down. Mr. Billy, too, 'cause he came lots of times to watch me practice and would say time and time again, "Atta girl Honey! Go get 'em." I 'specially liked havin' Mr. Billy root for me. When he rode O'Malley, his hair flew like the Swamp Fox's. I wanted my hair to fly that way too.

At our first practice session with all the new equipment, Ace set up an obstacle course just like I'd hafta run at Sportsman's, subject to the judge's final decisions. I got off to a ragged start—so ragged Ace didn't even bother to time me. I missed weaves in both weave poles, ducked the tire jump, and nearly fell off the dog walk. It was a sorry performance which made me wonder if I'd ever get the hang of it.

"Let's take a break," Ace told me. He 'splained that we'd never practice too long at one time. "Your attention span is intense Honey, but it can't last but so long. So, we'll take frequent breaks and let you rest up. I'm certain you'll get better and better the more we do this. Just be patient."

It helped hearin' him say that, and the next time I ran the course I *did* get a little bit better. I sailed right through the tire jump and didn't falter one bit on the dog walk. Even so, I missed weaves on both weave poles.

"Much better," Ace shouted. "You came close to knockin' my curveball out of the ballpark." I felt much better, but still it was a lot to remember—and he hadn't even timed me with his stopwatch.

The third time I ran the course Ace timed me. I still faulted on the weave poles once again and took one jump the wrong way but otherwise was perfect. But my heart sank when Ace called out, "Fifty-two seconds. Got to cut seventeen seconds off of that—that's all." I couldn't believe it. I'd never win at Sportsman's—not in a million years. I was really down, even had my tail 'tween my legs. Didn't help any when Ace told me he'd be runnin' on the course with me to give me voice and hand signals on which obstacles to take. He stood then in the center of the ring and pointed to the obstacles or yelled out their names. Naturally, I got confused and managed somehow to run through both tunnels backwards.

Miss Jane had watched my last run sittin' in a foldin' chair just a few steps off the course. She sensed how disappointed I was. "That's enough for today," she told Ace. "Let Honey relax. I'm taking her back to the house for a special treat."

I wondered what that might be. Much to my delight she was soon poppin' the top off a can of Purina Chow with real chicken. She fed me those finger-sized morsels one by one. I licked my lips when I finished like there wasn't a worry in the world. But that was just for show. Deep down I was stewin' inside, near certain I'd fall smack dab on my hiney at Sportsman's.

That evening I followed Mr. Billy to the barn when he gave O'Malley his oats. Ace soon showed up with a glum look.

"Got bad news from the game lab," he told Mr. Billy. "We'd better get every dingo we can out of the swamp before it's too late."

Mr. Billy took one look at me and said, "Let's talk about that later."

Had no idea why he said that, but it left me plenty worried.

17

Marvels of Conehead Mojo

That mouth-waterin' Purina Chow with real chicken wasn't the only treat I got 'cause the very next day Miss Jane and Mr. Billy took me to lunch at the Wilcox Hotel. Presidents, movie stars, and lots of famous folks have stayed there. It's widely known for fine food and easy livin'.

Miss Jane called the Wilcox Aiken's living room. "You'll fit right in, Honey. Just lie down in front of the fireplace. The guests will all adore seeing you there."

When we first drove up, I had to blink my eyes to make sure it was real, the place was *that* grand. I 'specially liked the tall columns in front with flags rippin' in the breeze. I knew straight off the Wilcox was bound to serve great eats. The lobby smelled like pine needles when they first green up, the fresh lime I sometimes whiff in Miss Jane's perfume. Somethin' else I really liked was the curly wood on the lobby walls. Mr. Billy called it "a good example of nature dabbling in abstract art." Did nature do any dabblin'? First I'd heard tell of that. Anyhow, Mister B said its curlycue patterns could pass for buried treasure maps and aren't found in any other type of wood.

We got the best seat in the house, right in front of the great stone fireplace, which had rows of flowers and ferns on both sides of the hearth. The place is over a hundred years old and crammed full of antiques. I was worried I might break one, so I laid down in front of the fireplace, just as Miss Jane suggested. 'Fore long the warm fire and the smell of fine food had me lickin' my lips.

"Is your dog thirsty?" the waiter asked.

"Would you mind bringing her some sparkling water?" Miss Jane asked. "We're taking a break from her training routine. I'm sure she'd like something special."

The waiter came back in a jiff with a fancy bottle. The waiter showed it to Miss Jane and Mr. Billy just like he had their bottle of wine.

"San Pellegrino," she beamed with satisfaction as the waiter poured some in a silver bowl. "It's fizzy water Honey—a special treat you've earned with all your hard work."

I took two laps and looked up in surprise. The water had a bubbly tang. "Drink up," Mr. Billy laughed. "Not many dogs get San Pellegrino."

Didn't want to hurt his feelin's but I'd take ditch water over that stuff anytime. But I sure wouldn't pass on the lunch—you don't get eats like that in the swamp, a thick burger cooked on the pink side. "It's pure Angus beef," said Miss Jane. "Even better than the Purina Chow with real chicken you like so much." As usual, she was right, she really was.

By then I'd forgot all about runnin' through the tunnels backwards. I wondered what if the pack could see me now, drinkin' from a silver bowl, a fine napkin 'round my neck. I knew Sugar would say I was puttin' on airs and Popeye was bound to say I was actin' like a big shot. But what could I say? The Wilcox was high cotton, just as Ace said—the kinda place where I forgot all about the taste of vole and grub.

Ace always said we were in high cotton when things were goin' just right. But to tell the truth, things coulda been a whole lot better. Somehow, I had to shave seventeen seconds off my time and run the course without a single fault. That tall order made me wonder: Can I really do it? As my doubts rose, my tail sank lower and lower, almost hid 'tween my legs. I kept thinkin' over and over: What if I let my second pack down? And the first one, too?

Sometimes you get a lift when least expected. On our way home from the Wilcox, we saw two men in yellow suits jump off a red truck with a ladder on the side. They hooked a hose to a hydrant that looked a lot like our coneheads in the swamp, only this one was red. Next, they shot a big spray out the nozzle that left the street clean as a whistle. At the very next stop light, I spied a dog peein' on a conehead. That told me when the men sprayed water out, the local dogs put it back—well, maybe not all the water but much as they could. I was sure our coneheads in the swamp could spray safety rays just like the hydrants in town.

And if I could catch a ray, I'd be runnin' as fast as the water sprayed by the men in the yellow suits. I decided to practice even harder, to do whatever it took to get my time under thirty-five seconds and not let Miss Jane down. Or the dingos in the swamp. Or Mr. Billy and Ace for that matter. That meant we'd all be simpatico with nothin' left to chance. The way Ace used that word it seemed to mean close and tight. I knew we'd have to be *simpatico* to win at Sportsman's. That was our goal, and we couldn't let anything stand in our way.

I musta caught a conehead ray 'cause good things started to happen right away. Two outstandin' experts on dog agility came all the way from Memphis at Miss Jane's request to coach Ace and me both. They were Rick and Jackie Lancaster who'd shown dingos for years. Two of their dogs, Star and Saigon, had won many agility championships, so Miss Jane wanted Rick and Jackie to help us improve.

They watched for a long while without sayin' a word, as Ace put me through my paces. Finally, Rick strolled over, squatted down, and rubbed my back. "Little girl, you've got all the natural talent anyone could hope for." Then, lookin' at Ace, he said, "I don't see a lot that needs changing other than your shoulder movements."

"Mine?" Ace asked in surprise.

"If your shoulders point the slightest bit off, that sends Honey the wrong signal. She may even run to the wrong obstacle. Hate to tell you this but most faults are caused by the handler—not the dog."

A mite embarrassed, Ace asked, "So what am I'm doin' wrong?"

"As I said, not much at all. Just keep your shoulders aligned with the obstacle you want Honey to take. She takes her cues from how you stand—that's the signal she reads. I'm sure she'll do *exactly* what you tell her."

It surprised me no end to hear what Rick said. I'd thought all along that the mistakes were all mine, never once thought that Ace might send me the wrong signal. My confidence went up a notch or two. Sure, I had to keep the old eagle eye on Ace, but if Rick was right, we'd get better and better fast.

After that we did a couple of walk-throughs with Ace aligning his shoulders to every obstacle on the course.

"You time us," Ace said handin' the stopwatch to Rick.

"Okay, show me what you can do . . . now go!" Once Rick yelled that out, I took off like I'd been shot out of a cannon. Ace pointed his shoulders perfectly and I zipped 'round the course without makin' even one fault.

"Forty-one seconds," Rick announced. "You shaved off eleven seconds. I'd never have believed such an improvement."

"Nothin' can stop us now, Honey," Ace beamed. "A run like that makes you feel like a million bucks."

Musta not been thinkin' when he said that 'cause I can't count that high. But it did feel mighty good, almost as good as a Wilcox burger served in a fine silver bowl. On top of the world, Ace would later say, and that's exactly what I felt like.

After five days of coachin', the Lancasters left, but by then we'd reached a whole new level. With the practical pointers

Jackie and Rick gave, plus my improved confidence, we knew the thirty-five-second mark was bound to fall—and soon.

They left on Sunday, and on Tuesday we lowered the time to thirty-nine seconds . . . down to thirty-seven seconds on Thursday. On Saturday, Mr. Billy took the stopwatch. I took the first set of weave poles so smoothly I surprised us all. After the first tunnel and a hard left turn, Ace lined up the tire jump and I sailed through with room to spare. I knew right then we had a great run in the makin'. After Ace sent me over the dog walk and the last bar jump, I hopped up onto the platform at the finish line without a single fault.

Mr. Billy leaped to his feet and threw both arms in the air. "You did it, Honey. You did it in thirty-four seconds. Fantastic!" Ace was first to hug my neck, but Miss Jane and Mr. Billy were close behind.

"We're on our way sweetheart." Miss Jane's tone of voice told me she was very, very happy. "You're only going to get better and better. Remember: practice makes perfect, especially when a doggie tries as hard as you do."

Later when we were all alone, Ace asked, "You don't have any religion, do you Honey?"

I gave him a puzzled look.

"Well, I guess it's okay for you to be a heathen. But I'm a Hard Shell Baptist myself, the foot-washin' kind. I'm thinkin' maybe I should wash your paws. After all, they're gonna carry us to the championship, that's how much faith I've got in you."

First time I'd heard him mention faith, but if faith meant strong believin', then I could feel it too. Somethin' *had* changed inside me. For the first time I believed I could win, that no spell cast by the Sidewinder, or even Geronimo, could stop us. Conehead mojo was with us—its marvels were there to see.

Not long after that Ace heard through the grapevine that Topper Guy was mouthin' off at Scooter's over how he bested the dog lady for a second time. He said she was dumb enough to bet that her good-for-nothin' ditch dog would win the Sportsman's Agility Championship. If she lost, she'd owe him her prize stud horse, Maestro Magic. The Sidewinder was offerin' a discount stud fee, but there weren't any takers yet.

"That crowd of his can't tell the difference between a prize mare and a plug mule," Ace scoffed.

Ragtop had asked Topper Guy what he'd do if Miss Jane won.

"That's the dumbest question I've ever heard," Topper Guy shot back.

"Okay, but that lady ain't in it to lose."

"Duh—doncha think I know that? She ain't got a chance when push comes to shove. That stud horse is mine. So, put that in your pipe and smoke it."

Ace gave me a big wink when we heard that. "That's not the kind of confidence we want, Honey. Ours is built on hard work and constant practice. The Good Book says, 'Pride goeth before destruction' and I'm tellin' you the Sidewinder is goin' off the high dive into a pool without one drop of water."

18

Houdini Escape

The Sportsman's Agility Championship was only a week away when Miss Jane decided I needed a final tune-up. Much to my surprise she aimed to take me to a hunt with the Mount Vintage Foxhounds. Ace was dead set against it, thinkin' that a foxhunt was bound to confuse me. As he put it, "It's tough enough for Honey to wiggle through her weave poles. I don't think racin' through the woods with a pack of hounds will help her at all."

"Ordinarily I'd agree," Miss Jane replied. "But a change of pace will do Honey good. Running long stretches at top speed will help her stamina, and a live hunt will put her on the lookout for the unexpected." She felt strongly about that 'cause the judges at Sportsman's were bound to spring surprises in how various courses got set up. After hearin' all that, Ace scratched his head just a bit and said, "Well, I guess you might as well take her."

The very next day we joined a caravan of hunters, horses, and hounds on the half-hour drive from Aiken to Mount Vintage Plantation near Edgefield. I rode in the pickup with Ace, who told me 'bout the uptight Yankees who came south for foxhuntin'. He called 'em "new rich that love to strut and love to show off what they've got. And mind you, they'll bark at you if you don't do things to suit 'em." After hearin' that, I thought maybe I'd sneak under the truck and take myself a nice long nap. Soon as we stopped, I crawled underneath the truck on my side, but Ace saw me. "Don't think you're getting away with that," he told me. "Just stay inside the truck 'til I call and be sure to buck up to run hard." Best I could figure, buck up meant the same as "grit your teeth" or gettin' down to business, as Mr. Billy often said.

Ace was right. The ruckus at the start made me so dizzy I didn't know which way to turn. Never seen so many horses, riders, and hounds balled up in one big knot. Ace counted nearly forty riders and even more dogs—all Penn-Marydels two times my size. They were white with black and brown spots. Hunters love 'em for their musical voices and ability to track. When the Penn-Marydels weren't sniffin' noses and fannies, they were bayin' and bawlin'—just itchin' to take off down the scent track.

Mr. Billy and his close friend, Mr. Bettis Rainsford, stood out in the bright red coats that hunt masters and field masters wear. Mr. Billy was ridin' O'Malley and, as usual, looked like the Swamp Fox all primed for the charge. Mr. Bettis was mounted on Charger, a dark bay draft built more for power than speed. On the edge of the knot I saw Miss Jane on St. Cecelia, a beautiful bay mare. She had on a red coat and looked mighty pert in her black velvet cap and white gloves. She pointed to where five youngsters sat on small ponies and told Ace: "Put Honey in back with the pony brigade. She can go full speed once the chase begins." At that, he lowered my window and I jumped out. Soon as I did, a bunch of nosy Penn-Marydels rushed over and started sniffin' me. They got so fresh Ace ran 'em off with a stick.

"Just can't help it," he laughed. "Their sniffers never stop." He said a Penn-Marydel's stamina is second to none, but they aren't that fast. "Don't worry Honey, you can run circles 'round those mutts. Anyway, they'll follow the scent sock 'til they get on the trail of a coyote."

Sure enough, a horseman soon took off draggin' a sock doused with coyote urine. Once he disappeared down the trail, Mr. Bettis blew his brass hunting horn to signal giddy up and go. The horn had a coiled tube that sounded rich notes that brought all the churnin' and sniffin' to a halt. As Hunt Master, Mr. Bettis rode off first with Mr. Billy, the Field Master, five or six horse lengths behind. His job was to control the hounds whose long ears were just above the scent track. Ace told me earlier that their ears trap the scent for their noses.

The fastest riders, just itchin' to take all those risky jumps, came right behind the dogs. The riders who were just learnin' the ways of fox huntin' came next. They'd steer clear of the jumps and watch how the expert riders performed. Last came the pony brigade: Miss Jane's grandson, Thomas Nelson, age ten, his cousins, Victoria Bedford, eight, Harrison Bedford, seven, and two family friends, Buckley Randolph and Philip Rutledge, both twelve. They'd come with their ponies all the way from Virginia. I was glad to see that Jack, a friend of theirs from Aiken, was riding a Marsh Tacky pony, a rare breed brought to South Carolina by Spanish explorers way back when. Because they adapted well to coastal lowlands, Marsh Tackies were ridden in Revolutionary War battles. Today the breed, like ours, is threatened with extinction.

Have to say the take-off on a bright fall afternoon was a sight to behold—riders on gallopin' steeds, a choir of happy hounds, and kids bouncin' along on fat little ponies. The frontrunners had to jump what local folks call "an Aiken"—a stack of logs covered with bushes and briars. That seemed safer than the stone walls they jump up north. At the very first Aiken we came up on a matron dustin' off her backside. When she fell, her mount had run off and left her. Through clenched teeth she vowed to send the nag to the glue factory first chance she got. Might have been an uptight Yankee for all I know. I just hoped she'd calm down and keep her poor horse in oats.

Pretty soon we left the high ground where the plantation house once stood. The hunt then entered wild terrain along Burkhalter Creek, a fast-movin' stream between steep ridges covered with pines. A wildlife trail ran 'longside the creek through old growth hickory and oak, but the horses and riders had to follow an old loggin' trail on the other side of the stream where traction was poor due to recent rains.

'Fore long I got tired of lookin' at pony backsides and started itchin' to move up front. Ace had warned that the Penn-Marydels will attack any dog that horns in on their hunt. I asked myself, *Should I take that risk?* I'd been sniffed out by a curious few at the start—not the pack leaders, who were bound to think I was buttin' in. I was stewin' over this when the hounds picked up a strong coyote scent. At the time, the coyote was nappin' in tall grass just off the loggin' trail but woke up when the yappin' got close and took off upstream on the wildlife trail. As the scent got stronger and stronger, the hounds' voices changed from yips and yelps to high-pitched bawls. An all-out chase was underway with the Penn-Marydels runnin' now at top speed.

Right away the voices of the older, experienced hounds told Mr. Bettis and Mr. Billy the hunt had entered a dangerous new stage. Once the hounds took after a coyote, they'd be hard to control. The horses were excited too, which greatly concerned the head huntsmen. It'd only take one slip on the muddy loggin' road to cause a bad spill—one where horses and riders both got hurt, maybe badly. Last but not least, they sensed from the first that this was not just any coyote. The hounds sounded hysterical, which told them they'd chased this one before—that it had to be Geronimo.

In back with the pony brigade, all I knew was the hounds had to be closin' in on somethin'. Just then a rider came toward us holdin' the reins of a second horse whose saddle was empty. Must belong to the lady who fell, I thought. The rider yelled as he passed, "They say a big coyote named Geronimo is ahead of the hounds by just a few seconds. They're going to pin him down at No Name Dam and tear him apart."

"Tally ho!" one of the kids yelled. "We don't want to miss that."

The words *tear him apart* made my neck fur rise. I knew Geronimo had done some bad things, that he might have killed the pets in Aiken. But tear him to pieces? Twelve American Dingos had paid for that with their necks. Bad as that was, I still didn't want the hounds to do their worst. After all, he was next of kin, a fellow wild dog. Dingos and coyotes had even mated to give birth to what Papa called coydogs. Others in the swamp practiced kill or be killed, but Mama and Papa preached "Always try to live and let live. It's the first commandment of a dingo." The Great Spirit first gave it to the Cherokees in the legend of Little Deer, who taught the tribe to live in harmony with others—to show respect especially for the deer they hunted and killed.

Coyotes don't kill for pleasure, so I figured Geronimo might know 'bout Little Deer too. Anyhow, I was sure live and let live meant nothin' to the Penn-Marydels—if they got their way they'd drain every last drop of Geronimo's blood.

Gotta help him somehow! That thought started ringin' in my ears and set my heart to poundin'. While I was tryin' to decide what to do, Geronimo made a darin' move at Shelving Rock, where the creek narrows down. He plunged into its racin' waters, scrambled up the far bank, and started runnin' back downstream.

In just seconds, he got around the shocked hounds that were runnin' upstream on the loggin' road—that turned the whole hunt upside down. Mr. Bettis and Mr. Billy did their best to calm things down but, unfortunately, the hounds and horses all tried to turn back at once. A few hounds plunged into the stream and tried to get past the confused knot and chase Geronimo downstream. Others spooked the horses by scramblin' under their hooves. That caused several horses and riders to go "ass over tea kettle," as Mr. Billy would later say. "We had a riot on our hands—one of the worst mix-ups you can imagine. It was pure luck that no one got busted up or badly injured."

To confuse things even more, the hounds that crossed the creek picked up the scent of a herd of deer runnin' just ahead of Geronimo. The deer also crossed the creek at Shelving Rock just ahead of the coyote when they heard the hounds drawin' close. They were now runnin' downstream with a large buck in back to protect against predators. We were mighty lucky that the mixed scents slowed the hounds down just a bit.

Moments before the pile-up happened, Miss Jane went back to check on the pony brigade. When the field reversed, she heard the Penn-Marydels' voices change from the roar of the chase to howls of confusion. She knew somethin' had gone wrong. Suddenly, she saw Geronimo on her side of Burkhalter Creek and that told her the hunt had reversed course, and that the pony brigade was smack dab in the way and could get run over.

All bedlam was ringin' in my ears as she galloped toward us. She knew if the ponies got spooked, the kids could get thrown and trampled with the whole hunt comin' their way. Her instincts told her to make Geronimo disappear, so she cupped her hands and yelled "Picket line . . . picket line." The youngsters knew exactly what that meant. They quickly formed a line from the logging trail down the slope and onto the far side of Burkhalter Creek with each rider several pony lengths apart. They turned then to face Miss Jane just as Geronimo came into sight. That left his path forward blocked. If he turned to either side, the hounds would catch him. "Geronimo just ran out of real estate," Ace said at the end of the hunt.

I still don't know how Miss Jane doped it all out so quick, but she shouted, "Go to ground, Honey! There . . . there!" She pointed toward a huge pile of treetops and limbs soon to be burned. I knew straight off that she wanted me to hide in that pile and hoped that Geronimo would follow. Go to ground meant end the chase. She wanted the hunt over without a moment's delay. As I wormed my way into the pile, Geronimo followed right behind me.

We'd barely got inside when Miss Jane jumped off her horse and called, "Come quick, Honey!" I heard fear in her voice but did what she asked, even though the Penn-Marydels were bearin' down with crazed looks. When I poked my head out, she grabbed me by the collar, "Now go, Honey . . . go!" She pointed away from the hounds. "Run, girl—run as fast as you can!"

I took off like a bolt outta the blue. When the hounds saw me, they went loco—they were dead certain I was Geronimo—that finally they would catch me and tear me apart instead. But, just as Ace predicted, I could run circles 'round any Penn-Marydel. In the chase that followed they had no chance at all. Pretty soon, all I could hear was their disappointed yips and yowls.

After a bit Mr. Billy, Mr. Bettis, and the whippers-in caught up with the hounds and called 'em off. "Leave it . . . leave it," they yelled over and over again. With whips poppin' just above their ears, the hounds finally called it quits. I kept my distance from

The Penn-Marydels chase me thinkin' I'm Geronimo.

the Penn-Marydels as the hunt moseyed back down the trail to the trucks and trailers parked at the startin' point.

When I trotted up to Ace's truck, Miss Jane made a bee line to meet me. "Honey, you were so brave. You were wonderful! You're the smartest dog in the whole wide world." Wasn't so sure 'bout that, but my chest puffed out anyway. She musta told Mr. Billy and Ace what I'd done 'cause they were beamin' too. Mr. Billy kept sayin' "Great job, Honey—great job!" And Ace told me, "I knew you could run like greased lightning. Know what? That was a Houdini escape you just pulled."

After the hunt Miss Jane's daughter, Jane Page Thompson, and her husband Mark, hosted a hunt breakfast at their home called The Gallop. She served a fancy buffet of beaten biscuits and Virginia ham with a hot casserole and hot cider that I heard had been spiked with whiskey. It was a chilly day, so some said the whiskey went down easy. I was happy 'cause Jane Page and Mark both gave me a ham biscuit. After that I cuddled up on the couch with Miss Jane. She told me, "I want you to remember the lessons from today's hunt. First of all, the unexpected can happen at any time—most often when we least expect. And second, things often are not what they seem. The hounds were absolutely certain that you were Geronimo, but they were dead wrong."

She said I'd saved Geronimo's neck and helped prevent a worse riot. But I didn't think the credit should all go to me by a long shot. The youngsters had been mighty brave to set up that picket line. Their actions reminded Miss Jane to tell me 'bout a famous incident at Shelving Rock during the Revolutionary War. The Tories were scourin' the countryside to find George Miller Jr., who'd been wounded in a battle. He wasn't much more'n a boy, but they aimed to hang him anyway. His sister, Annsybil, decided to hide him at Shelving Rock and carried food to him there in a water bucket. He soon recovered and rejoined the fight for independence.

Miss Jane had known what to do when the riot was 'bout to break out. And she'd been right all along 'bout what I'd learn at the hunt. No judge at Sportsman's, or anywhere else, could ever set up an obstacle course like the one I had run that day at Mount Vintage Plantation.

The next mornin' Mr. Billy and Ace were feedin' up at the barn when a wildlife service truck pulled up. A game warden got out and handed them some papers. I noticed how grim they both looked.

"The toxicology report from our lab," the warden said. "It says the cause of death was poison."

"They poisoned those puppies?" Ace asked.

The game warden nodded. "Didn't stand a chance."

"I knew it. You could see the pain in their little faces."

As he examined the report, Mr. Billy suddenly exclaimed, "Ethylene glycol!"

"What the heck is that?" Ace asked.

"Antifreeze," the game warden answered. "One teaspoon's enough. It's that deadly."

"It's sweet to the taste—right?" Mr. Billy asked with a frown.

"That's why animals drink it. They're completely defenseless. In half an hour or less they seem groggy or drunk. By then it's already too late. The only hope is to get to a vet damn quick. Of course, they didn't have that option."

"This explains why those poor pups were desperate for water," Ace observed.

"Yes, thirst comes with vomiting and heavy breathing. At the end the kidneys fail, and the victim goes into a coma. I'd say it's the most painful death we can imagine."

"Who the hell would do such a thing?" Mr. Billy asked in anger.

"Can't say just yet. Your guess may be as good as mine."

19

The Grand Championship

Just 'fore we left, I heard Ace crowin' that we'd be the coolest cats of all up at Sportsman's. Had they entered me as a big-eared Siamese, I wondered? What he meant was we'd all be dressed to the nines 'cause of our new doodad. The doodad was a crest Miss Jane got made up for Banbury Cross Farm. Ace had one on his shirt—toenail-sized, he called it—with a lot packed into that small space, a red cap like a jockey wears over red and white racin' stripes.

Mr. Billy said to think of the crest as our coat of arms.

"Sounds a tad snooty," Ace told me off to one side. He said the proper coat of arms for any self-respectin' dingo would be crossed soup bones. That sounded just right to me.

The doodad was even painted on the doors of the trucks we were drivin' north. My new collar sported a doodad and so did Mr. Billy's necktie. Despite what Ace said, the thingamajigs did make us look mighty snappy—like world-beaters, I thought.

On the trip north, Mr. Billy drove the first truck and Miss Jane sat up front. Ace sat in back with me. Asa, who was Ace's assistant, followed in a second truck with all our equipment, includin' a crate (which I can't stand). Ira, who helps Ace run the kennel, rode with Asa. All the dingos love Ira 'cause he carries treats in his pockets.

On the ride up I wasn't one bit nervous until Ace happened to say, "Honey, don't be surprised if you see Topper Guy and Ragtop once we get there."

That sorry pair hadn't crossed my mind, but I knew they'd be rootin' for me to fall off the A-frame smack dab on my hiney. When he saw my worried look, Ace said, "Guess I coulda gone all day without sayin' that. Sorry Honey—didn't mean to upset you."

I saw Mr. Billy watchin' me in the mirror . . . he had a twinkle in his eye. He soon broke out in a boomin' voice:

> To be, or not to be, that is the question:
> Whether 'tis Nobler in the mind to suffer
> The Slings and Arrows of outrageous Fortune,
> Or to take Arms against a Sea of troubles,
> And by opposing end them?

"Hamlet: Act 3, Scene 1," he added.

The words rang true. I did have a sea of troubles, but how would I take arms against the Sidewinder?

Mr. Billy then told Ace, "We need to lighten up. Do you know the words to 'Wabash Cannonball'?" They got out a few lines but soon gave up. "What about this one?" Mr. Billy said with a big laugh.

> Yeah, they ran through the briars and they ran through the brambles
> And they ran through the bushes where a rabbit couldn't go.
> They ran so fast that the hounds couldn't catch 'em
> Down the Mississippi to the Gulf of Mexico.

"What's that?" Ace asked.

"'Battle of New Orleans,'" Mr. Billy replied. "The hounds couldn't catch the British and no one's going to catch Honey at Sportsman's. She's a champion and will outrun 'em all."

"Okay guys, that's enough," Miss Jane cut in. "Honey's going to be just fine. Don't make her nervous."

When we arrived at the Purina Farms' Event Center outside St. Louis, we were amazed by how big it was and the spiffy facilities there for national dog agility shows.

"This has gotta be one of the best in the country," Mr. Billy told us.

"Told you we'd get you to the big leagues," Ace laughed, rubbing my neck and ears.

It was almost too much for me to take in with its brightly painted buildings, tree-lined parking areas, and lush green agility fields.

The first runs of the three-day championship were set for that afternoon. My spirits soared when I saw that Rick and Jackie had come all the way from Memphis to cheer for me. Rick and Juanita Oser had come from Wilmington to do the same. Like the Lancasters, the Osers had competed with several American Dingos bred by Miss Jane. After greetin' our cheerin' section, Ace walked me on the arena floor to give me a feel for sprint turf. It felt 'bout like the rug in Miss Jane's livin' room. It'd be easy to run on. The judges soon called the handlers to the arena floor to explain how they aimed to set up the obstacle courses.

"You stay here while I take care of this," Ace said, loopin' my leash around a fence post. I stretched out on the turf to watch, feelin' relaxed and ready for my first run. Just then a voice behind me sneered: "Hey loser—why'd you even bother to come? You ain't got no business bein' at such a fancy arena. Did you forgit you belong in a ditch?"

I turned and saw Topper Guy leanin' over the fence with Ragtop peepin' over his shoulder. The Sidewinder gave me a hard glare. "You sorry no good stray. You ain't got a chance. I'd be ashamed to even bring you up here."

Hearin' his snarky voice was . . . well, it felt like I'd stepped on a gator log—no tellin' what kind of vicious swipe he'd take next.

I glanced around the stands hopin' Miss Jane or Mr. Billy would see seem them tryin' to torment me. I wanted them to chase off that sorry pair in the worst way, but Miss Jean and Mr. Billy had their backs turned. They had no idea my worst fear had hit me. When I turned back to look again, the Sidewinder and his sidekick had gone. They'd come outta nowhere and took off just as quick.

Ace came back full of glowin' optimism. "Piece of cake Honey. The course is set up just the way we like it. You're goin' to be just great." He noticed then how I had my tail stuck between my legs.

"Hey, what's wrong, girl? Somebody upset you?"

I wanted to tell him in the worst way 'bout the Sidewinder's nasty words. I shot glances all around the arena, but the two rascals were nowhere to be seen. "Please tell me, little girl. Who're you looking for?"

Just then the master's flight was announced over the loudspeaker. So we lined up with the other handlers and dogs at the gate. "Don't worry Honey," Ace said rubbin' my back, "you'll be just fine once we start our run."

We were scheduled to run third behind two border collies. After watchin' their runs I began to think the Sidewinder might be right. Maybe I *was* in the wrong place. The border collies ran fault-free times that'd be hard to beat. By the time my turn came, my stomach was in knots. I ran in a cautious, make-no-mistakes way ("tiptoeing on eggshells," Ace later said). I was way too slow on the A-frame and tire jump, and for the first time ever (I still don't know why) I ran through the first tunnel backwards. By the time I went back and did it right, my time for the entire run was shot. It soon got posted on the board: forty-five seconds, my worst run in weeks. The Border Collies were a mile ahead. I'd dug a hole so deep I'd never climb out.

In two more runs that afternoon I made more dumb mistakes. When we left for the day, I had fallen so far behind Petey, the top

Border Collie, we all knew it'd take a miracle to catch up. Made me sick to think of the Sidewinder winnin' Maestro Magic, Miss Jane's champion stud horse—and me goin' back to Aiken with my tail 'tween my legs for good.

When we got to our hotel Mr. Billy told Ace a judge had overheard Topper Guy talkin' mean to me.

Ace smacked a hand to his forehead. "I knew it! I knew somethin' had to be holdin' her back. That no account rascal! Just wait 'til I get my hands on him."

"Don't bother. I asked the arena to throw him out, but they can't unless we can prove what he did. That's next to impossible. Instead, we've got to get Honey relaxed—focused on her runs and ignorin' any more taunts he makes."

"That's a tall order," Ace said. "I'll take her up to the room and get her settled down."

"No—hold off on that. Jane wants to feed her and have a heart-to-heart talk."

A bit later Miss Jane took me to her room and gave me a bowl full of chow, but I was way too upset to eat. "If you're not going to touch your food, then come here." She held out her hand and I jumped on the bed, so we could curl up together. I s'pose my look told her how sorry I was that I'd let her down. I felt so low and wondered how I could ever make it up to her.

"Don't worry, sweetheart. It's not the end of the world, even if we don't win Sportsman's. You'll still be precious, and no one can *ever* take that away." After that Miss Jane made me happy and relaxed, as she had so many times before, with her sing-song verses 'bout "Honey the funny bunny." I 'specially liked one line: "And here's a sigh for that rascal Topper Guy, who will cry, cry, and cry when he sees how fast Honey can fly." Amazin' how much better her words—what she called "nonsense rhymes"—made me feel.

The next mornin' I felt a lot better, but the closer we got to the arena the more I worried 'bout more bad runs. I just couldn't

119

let Miss Jane down—or all the strays, as the Sidewinder called us. Somehow, I had to avoid the dumb mistakes I'd made the day before.

The first time out, Petey ran another fault-free run in thirty-four seconds. Ace and I were waitin' for the start signal when I spied Topper Guy and Ragtop in the first row behind the gate. When he saw me lookin' his way, he reached over and grabbed Ragtop by the throat like he'd choke him to death. After a spine-chillin' laugh, he pointed at me and shouted, "You . . . you . . . you."

When he heard those taunts, Ace turned and saw the Sidewinder with his hands around Ragtop's throat. I could tell he was boilin' mad. "Honey, that son of a gun thinks you're a choker. So, show him there ain't a chokin' bone in your body." When he said that, somethin' inside me snapped. My neck fur rose and the words of Mr. Billy's quote came back: I had to oppose my sea of troubles in order to end 'em.

Later on, Ace said I took off like I was shot out of a cannon. I bounded up the A-frame at top speed, sailed through the tire jump, and threaded the first weave pole like an eel slippin' through sea grass. My cuts were so quick the course was a blur. The last obstacle was the dog walk over a narrow plank—the high wire of agility. I'd been very cautious up to now, but this time I bounded across without the slightest fear of fallin'. When I came down the ramp, I knew I had what Ace called a hot time. They soon posted on the scoreboard that I'd run a fault-free run of thirty-three seconds. I'd whipped Petey on the standard course for the first time.

Miss Jane blew kisses and Mr. Billy gave me the V-sign as I left the arena floor. The others in my cheerin' section yelled and waved their arms. When I peeked at Topper Guy, he was slumped in his seat like his mama just smacked him. My confidence jumped way up 'cause I knew right then I could whip Petey and take that championship home to Aiken.

Ace says I looked like I got shot out of a cannon at the race of my life.

That afternoon I ran my best time ever on a standard course at twenty-nine seconds. It also was the best time posted at the trials and tied me with Petey at the top of the leaderboard. The championship would be decided on Sunday in a Jumpers event that would be a tough test of how well Ace and I worked together.

When we got back to the hotel Miss Jane suggested that we all turn in early and get a good night's rest. She took me to her room and was mighty tickled that my appetite had come back. No wonder: she popped the top on a can of Purina Chow with real chicken. Next mornin' when we got back to the arena, I felt a new bounce in my step which I needed. The jumpers require very quick cuts and a time limit of twenty-seven seconds.

The atmosphere was full of tension and excitement when Petey and I made our final runs. People were jammed at the rails and cheerin' loud as we made our cuts and jumps. We stayed neck and neck until Petey slowed just a bit comin' out of the last turn. That caused his hind leg to drag just a bit and he knocked down a bar—the eighteenth and final one on the course. It was his first fault of the day. I still had none, but he was still ahead in terms of timing, by a fraction of a second.

As we waited for the start signal for our final run, Ace told me: "Okay, this is the moment we've been waiting for." Then, with a big grin he added, "If we can just stay in sync in still mode, you'll be the new champion." I knew I had to listen extra hard 'cause his directions told me where to cut and when to jump. In still mode he'd stand in the middle of the course and barely move at all so as to eliminate any confusion caused by body movement. We'd practiced still mode but had never tried it on a course like Sportsman's.

Afterward people would say that run showed crystal clear just how strong the bond 'tween a dog and a handler can be. Ace's voice signals came through loud and clear. His hand signals did too. Without movin' more'n a step or two he signaled exactly what I needed to know. I got through all eighteen jumps without a single fault and bested Petey's time by 1.45 seconds. Despite my terrible start on the first day, I had just won the Sportsman's Agility Championship.

I had barely finished when Miss Jane and Mr. Billy came runnin' out onto the obstacle course. She knelt down and gave me a big kiss . . . Mr. Billy kept sayin' "Great job, Honey!" over and over. They both hugged Ace and told him how masterful his performance was. By then we were surrounded by flashin' cameras and the crowd.

I was the happiest dog in the world when they gave me the blue ribbon. My only wish was that Mama, Papa, Sugar, and Popeye could see me now. I knew they'd be bustin' out with pride, just like my people pack. We'd be goin' back to Aiken with a championship—not in disgrace like Topper Guy had predicted.

Even more'n that ribbon I wanted to see the Sidewinder hand over that gun he came so near to shootin' me with. He'd said on the first day he'd meet us in the parkin' lot once everything was over. After the awards ceremony ended, we went back to the truck to meet him and Ragtop, but they weren't there.

"Let's give 'em a few more minutes," Mr. Billy said.

We waited and waited—a half hour or more. Finally, Mr. Billy started the truck and said in disgust, "Let's go."

Ace gave me a knowin' look. "Why am I not surprised?" he said. "I never figured the Sidewinder for a man of his word."

I was mighty disgusted with those sorry critters for not showin' up. I wanted to see how whipped they'd look, especially after all the mean things they'd done to me.

20

A Champion's Life

Ace had predicted that Aiken would give me a hero's welcome, and the town sure did. More'n anything, Aiken reveres its champion horses *and* its blue ribbon dogs, so the good folk there opened their hearts to me. I got my picture in the paper, and so did Miss Jane, Mr. Billy, and Ace. The mayor made me an honorary citizen and gave me a key to the city. Later, Ace told me, "Don't bother worryin' 'bout lockin' the city up. That key's just another feather in your cap." I figured Ace musta forgot I don't wear caps 'cause of my ears. Still, I figured the key *had* to be worth a little somethin'. Maybe it'd get me inside the Bi-Lo, where they had a whole shelf of that delicious Purina Chow with real chicken.

After the ceremony Miss Jane and Mr. Billy took me on a long walk among the longleaf pines in Hitchcock Woods. As we strolled among the trees, Mr. Billy quoted a few of his favorite lines:

A wet sheet and a flowing sea,
A wind that follows fast,
And fills the white and rustling sail,
And bends the gallant mast.

I become an honorary citizen and get a key to the City of Aiken.

Pointing to a tree reaching toward the clouds, he said, "Now there indeed is a gallant mast. Fit for a four-masted clipper hauling tea from China. Imagine how it swayed in the Straits of Magellan. You know about the stormy straits at the bottom of South America, don't you Honey?"

Hated to, but all I could give him was a dumb look.

"The tip of South America. World's most dangerous passage for sailors. And what kept the tea dry deep in the hull? Tar and pitch from these very pines made it leak-proof." Then, Mr. Billy sadly shook his head. "Takes over a hundred years to grow a longleaf pine and it can last for five hundred years, but man can cut 'em down in minutes. The longleaf brought the world to our door. But alas, the gallant masts could not last."

After that Miss Jane and Mr. Billy talked over what I should do next. "You'll soon turn two," Mr. Billy said. "If you continue to compete in agility, you can be one of the greatest champions ever."

Miss Jane sniffed a bit at those words. "I don't feel that she's got a thing left to prove in agility. She won in a pressure cooker despite Topper Guy's taunts and threats. She's already a great champion. I'm more interested in her bloodline."

"Meaning puppies?" Mr. Billy asked.

Suddenly it dawned on me that Miss Jane wanted me to have a litter. Me, a mother? What a scary idea! I wondered who I'd mate with. Hopefully, someone as good and kind as Papa. If I did have puppies, I'd want to keep 'em all—just like Mama and Papa. I thought Miss Jane might let me. After all, she and Mr. Billy were savin' the dingo breed from extinction . . . and that was why there were so many dingos at Banbury Cross Farm. Then, the thought hit me that they could only keep so many.

People were comin' all the time to get a puppy, offerin' good homes and a lovin' family. They'd have to give any pipsqueak of mine lots of love or answer to me *and* Miss Jane. She put the eagle eye on every would-be owner and turned down all whose true intentions she doubted. One couple started arguin' after they wrote their check, so she tore it up and took the puppy back. She also saw to every detail. She had shipped pups all over the world. They all showed up in baggage claim with a huge red, white, and blue ribbon on their crate. The new owner couldn't possibly miss 'em.

Once we got back from Hitchcock Woods, I went to the Clipper to find Ace. He was there cuttin' up hot dogs.

"For the champ," he said, tossin' a slice to me. "Now what's this I hear about you havin' a litter of puppies?"

That meant he'd talked to Miss Jane. The subject made me real nervous . . . he could see that.

"Well, no one's goin' to rush you. That's all I'm sayin' on that subject."

He talked then 'bout my performance at Sportsman's—how it reminded him of his prize fights in his twenties. "They knocked me down plenty, but I always got back on my feet—just like you did, Honey. Those Border Collies knocked you down but couldn't knock you out. Like I said sometime back, you've got a mighty big heart."

Comin' from Ace, that felt like my second blue ribbon.

The next day I got the biggest surprise I've ever had. I was in the kitchen with Miss Jane and Mr. Billy when Ace came in.

"Some folks here to see you, Honey. They're waitin' out back."

When we got outside, I could hardly believe my eyes. Mama, Papa, Sugar, and Popeye were standin' on the edge of the lawn. I blinked in shock, thinkin' some phantom must have run 'em out of the swamp. Or that somebody had played a trick. But

What I dreamed of for so long—back with Mama, Papa, Sugar, and Popeye once again.

sure enough it was them, alive and well if nervous to be in such a strange place. Like me, they'd never left the swamp before.

We just stared at each other for what seemed like the longest while. Then, Mama whimpered in the tenderest way, like she thought she'd never see me again. Once she did that, I couldn't hold back for another instant. My feet barely touched the ground as I bounded to my alpha mom. The whole pack then melted into one big yellow ball of joy.

Ace said later he'd never heard so many happy yips and yelps. Or seen so many tender nuzzles and licks.

After I got rescued by Miss Jane, I lived in dread that my pack would all get trapped or shot. But here lately, all I could see was the dead deer with that wild-eyed look. I knew how it died and worried every day that one of my pack would turn up alongside the Critter Trail with foam on the mouth. That, I told myself, would be the cruelest death of all, but somehow Mama, Papa, Sugar, and Popeye had got through the crisis in the swamp.

A whole year had gone by and now, straight out of the blue, what I'd wished for the most had come true. The whole pack—our Super Pack, as Mr. Billy called it—was together, safe and sound. There was nothin'—absolutely nothin'—I could wish for more'n that.

Turned out that Mr. Billy and Ace had hired an old-timey trapper named Taylor Mayo to round up my next of kin. He'd put a bunch of traps with padded jaws (which won't break a leg) 'longside the Critter Trail. He'd baited the traps with pig's knuckle right out of the jar on the bar at Scooter's. One by one old Tom caught 'em: first Sugar, then Popeye, then Mama, and finally, after a week's wait, Papa. He kept 'em all in a pen in his yard 'til he caught Papa. After catchin' him, he brought them to the farm that same mornin'.

Ace asked the old trapper if he'd ever seen any happier dogs. "Guess not," the old codger replied. "But the main thing I see is loyalty."

"Hadn't thought about that," Ace replied.

"Well, look at it this way: s'pose by accident you locked your wife and your dog in the trunk of your car. When you opened it up, which one do you think would be glad to see you?"

"No doubt about that—the dog," Ace said with a big laugh. "Dogs can teach humans a whole lot 'bout loyalty."

After all was said and done, Papa was happy to lay his head down in a doghouse. He told us, "The swamp ain't as safe as it used to be—especially for those with a coyote look."

A few days later the game warden paid Mr. Billy and Ace a second visit. "Came out to let you know we've closed the case on who poisoned those animals back in the swamp."

"You caught somebody?" Ace asked.

"As a matter of fact, we have," the game warden replied.

"I hope you lock 'em up and throw the key away."

"As a matter of fact, the perpetrator will do hard time."

"Meaning what?" Mr. Billy asked.

"A year or more with no chance of parole."

"So, who'd you nail?" Ace demanded.

"A fellow named Topper Guy Sawyer. Ever hear of him?"

Mr. Billy and Ace gave each other knowing winks.

"Have we ever," Mr. Billy exclaimed. "That guy all but shot her." He pointed to me lying on the ground at his feet.

"I'd sure like to know how you caught him," Ace said.

"It was partly due to a lucky break. Mr. Sawyer got stopped half a mile down the road from Scooter's. Blew twice the legal limit on the breathalyzer, so the patrolman, who's a friend of mine, took him in. When he searched his truck, he found a five-gallon can of antifreeze . . . almost empty."

"Was that enough to tie him to the poisonings?" Ace asked skeptically.

"The patrolman had seen a notice we put out on the case a few days ago. He called me, so we conducted a search of the truck. We found plastic cups that matched those found in the swamp."

"Have you got enough evidence to convict him?" Mr. Billy asked.

"Maybe, or maybe not. But it doesn't matter because he decided to cooperate. We've got his confession."

"You've gotta be kiddin'," Ace exclaimed. "Why would he fess up?"

"He got boxed in. He's got a buddy named Ragtop . . ."

"We know him," Ace injected. "Ain't too bright."

"You got that right. Turns out he'd done a whole lot of talking around Scooter's. It became common knowledge there what this Topper Guy claimed to have done. We won't be prosecuting this fellow you call Ragtop because he's gonna testify against his buddy. Crooks never seem to stick together."

"So, all Topper Guy's loudmouth talk finally caught up with him?" Ace asked.

"I suppose so. He had to sell his firearms in order to post bail."

Mr. Billy and Ace traded winks.

"Guess that means Miss Jane won't be collectin' on her bet," Ace opined.

"What bet?" the game warden asked.

"Never mind," Mr. Billy replied. "At least he won't be shooting any more innocent dingos. Jane will be mighty relieved to know that."

As the game warden turned to go, Mr. Billy said, "One last question: Why do you think he did it?"

"I suspect it's a control issue. Some people kill for pure pleasure. They enjoy hurting animals or even people. This guy needs a psychological examination. He'll have plenty of time for that now."

I was mighty relieved to hear that it was Topper Guy and not Geronimo who killed for pure pleasure. To me, the Sidewinder wasn't a phantom of the swamp like the coyote and the dingo—he was a demon instead. With him caught it seemed like roses were comin' up everywhere I looked. At last the pack was all together and safe. What more could I ask? That was ten times better than bein' crowned champion at Sportsman's. Did I already say I'm the luckiest dog in the world?

21
Second-Chance Dog

Mr. Billy had many roles at Banbury Cross Farm: horseman, huntsman, and our pack leader at times, though he mostly left that job to Miss Jane. I quickly learned that to him the pack stood for family—those you can always count on. One of his favorite books was *The Law of the Jungle*, which states that "the strength of the Pack is the Wolf, and the strength of the Wolf is the Pack."

A long time back Mr. Billy had told me, "Pack is *your* word, Honey. Humans use 'family,' but both words mean the same. Without the pack we are weaklings, but with the pack we are strong—strong enough to overcome more than we can imagine."

My pack had grown to include him, Miss Jane, and Ace. They'd helped me overcome a lot, but the greatest thing they'd done was get my first pack back together. After that, Mr. Billy started callin' us a Super Pack—sayin' we'd always stick together. The grandest doghouse he and Miss Jane had ever built now stood just behind the Big House. The sign over the door said FAMILY OF HONEY. No wonder I felt so lucky.

My good fortune made me want to help Miss Jane and Mr. Billy any way I could to keep the dingos from becomin' extinct. Their goal was to give the ones in the wild a good home—to let folks know 'bout dingos out there in the swamps, savannahs, and lowlands where they went lookin' for food when they lost their Native American masters at the Mississippi River in 1839. Every now and then I can smell a low-banked fire where the Cherokees once slow-dried sides of meat. Somehow the smoke has seeped deep into my blood—no, make that into my wild genes, and thank goodness I've still got wild genes. Rest assured after all I've been through, I pay close attention to my genes now at all times.

After we got separated from the Native Americans, we had to learn to be wild dogs all over again—there was no other way to survive. The pack's ability to work together became more important than ever. Once again, we made our dens in the notches of fallen trees, spoke our own language with fish-hook tails, and followed the strong peckin' order our alpha moms demanded. They were smart, tough, demandin', and kind. Sure, if someone had to fight off a coyote or some other predator, Papa would do that while Mama found a safe place to hide us pups.

After all was said and done, I saw the phantom and Geronimo now in a whole different light. I once thought Geronimo was a phantom castin' an evil spell over the swamp from the high cliff at Silver Bluff. Now, I was sure he was howlin' a wounded cry. With no pack, and bein' all alone, he had nowhere else to run. He'd been trapped and trucked two thousand miles, chased all over a huge hunt pen, and had wandered then all the way to the gator-infested waters of the Great Savannah. And all that talk 'bout him scarin' that poor deer to death? It was just talk—nothin' more. All made up to run him out of the swamp, once and for all.

Problem was, where could Geronimo go? What could he eat? Starvin' as he was, maybe he had pounced on small pets in Aiken. But it wasn't his fault we got blamed, that twelve innocent dingos paid the price for his hunger. It's always easy to blame the least-known critter, and that made Geronimo target number one. Would I trust him alone in the dark? Only the dumbest of the dumb would do that. I've learned the hard way to be careful who you run with, and watch where you step.

That ole soap bubble dream popped once more when I left the swamp. It had popped many times after thirteen-foot gators chased me in my dreams. This time when it popped my wishful thinkin' about conehead mojo. I'd once been so certain that cypress knees beamed safety rays all through the swamp. Now I knew they didn't. The vibes in the swamp came instead from the Great Spirit, who taught the Native Americans the idea of live and let live. They, in turn, had passed that along to the dingos who guarded their campfires. Comin' down the line, I got it from Mama and Papa, who also passed on their creed: "Respect other critters great and small, and never take more than you need."

Let me remind you that we're the oldest dog breed in the swamp—in North America, too. I'm sure our genes kept us alive. Mixed in with our wild ones are the love and loyalty we also learned from the Native Americans. Even after they were taken away, we never stopped lovin' humans. Once we got cut off, we missed 'em even more. Miss Jane saw that right away in how I looked at folks. I didn't make eye contact in quick glances like other dogs. My gaze always held steady. It told Miss Jane my loyalty would last forever. Native Americans saw the Great Spirit in our eyes. That's why they took us on their journey through life and into the afterlife too. They knew our love would last, as we often say, for forever and a day.

Today, I've got more names than any dog out there: Dingo, Carolina Dog, Old Yeller—even Ditch Dog. On the way back from Sportsman's, Ace told me, "Honey, you've done somethin' for all the dogs without a home. You're a Second-Chance Dog who became the champ. You proved that at Sportsman's, and no one *ever* can take that from you. Swamp dogs and strays will always be proud of you and all your adventures."

So, if you're lookin' for a dog, don't forget the stray that needs a second chance—one like I got. The kinda home I'm sure you can give. If you really, really want a dingo, keep your eyes peeled 'longside the road where the cattails grow and the ditch lilies bloom, where the coneheads peep up just above the waterline under the bald cypress trees. Soon you'll hear a murmur in among the reeds, the Great Spirit sayin', once again, *Live and let live, take no more than you need, be kind to all critters great and small.*

If you look close enough, sooner or later you'll see a tail waggin' in the happiest of ways. Your heart will jump when you spot those deep brown eyes starin' at you. If you open up your heart, that dingo will bounce right in and you've got yourself a Second-Chance Dog.

I finally learned the truth about Conehead Mojo—it's just live and let live like the Great Spirit says.

When that happens, you'll know the true meanin' of *One for all and all for one*. You'll never forget that the strength of the Pack is the Wolf, and the strength of the Wolf is the Pack.

Always yours . . . from Honey with love.

About Honey

She was a Carolina Dog through and through: made distinctive by her tall, pointy ears, inquisitive amber eyes, and fish hook tail. A certain magnetism also set her apart—her steady, locked-on gaze, and an air of wisdom, if it's possible for a dog to possess such a faculty. Most of all, Honey was loving and kind; she bonded with us and our family—we became her pack.

Honey, who inspired this book, died peacefully on the evening of October 19, 2021, just short of her seventeenth birthday. The vet who performed last rites was as kind, understanding, and comforting as a parish priest. Even so, watching her slip away was excruciatingly painful, but that did nothing to diminish the happy, exciting, and, at times, hair-raising life she led. When she was three, Honey got bit on the foreleg by a large snake. Of all times, it occurred on a Sunday morning in the swamp where we lived at the time on the Intracoastal Waterway in Eastern North Carolina. Luckily, my wife, Betsy, reached our vet by phone within minutes after she came limping out of the woods.

"Bring her to the clinic right away, and I'll meet you there," he generously offered. He treated her with Benadryl, antibiotics, and pain medicine and told us he thought she'd recover. For the next three days, Honey barely moved. Early on the fourth morning, Betsy scrambled a plateful of eggs and put them on the floor beside her. She ate them with gusto, and we knew she would soon recover.

In 2010, Honey went with us to Warsaw, Poland for a year, while I researched a book. She joined in the life of the city by riding packed subways at rush hour and learning to ride escalators. A frightening incident occurred at Central Station Warsaw as we boarded a packed train to Krakow. When I stepped from the platform onto the steps of the train, Honey followed. But suddenly, someone stepped backward, causing Honey to lose her balance. She then fell between the platform and train to the track as the conductor blew his whistle to signal departure. Fortunately, her leash and collar held as I pulled her up to the platform to safety. Honey was so shaken by the mishap that she insisted on sitting in a seat between us all the way to Krakow.

She and Betsy flew back from Poland together, but they missed their connection in Frankfurt. The airline told Betsy they'd have to stay there overnight—that she'd stay in a hotel and Honey would stay in a kennel. For reasons never explained, Honey got put right away on a flight to Dulles Airport, where she sat on arrival without food or water for almost 12 hours. A kind woman passing through the luggage area noticed that Honey didn't have a food or water bowl and called our daughter, Jennifer, whose name and phone number were listed on the crate. She drove from her home in Arlington to Dulles and picked Honey up. Sometime later, she went back to pick up Betsy, knowing she'd be distraught not to find Honey at baggage claim. Jennifer stood in from the automatic doors between baggage claim and the lobby and finally spied Betsy.

"Hey Mom . . . I've got Honey," she yelled. A happy reunion then followed.

I had looked forward very much to taking Honey to bookstore events once *From Honey with Love* got released. I had a stamp made of her paw print and planned to have Honey use it to "autograph" books. She will be with us in spirit, so I still plan to use the paw print stamp at book events.

I don't think we could ever fully say goodbye to Honey. She is too much a part of us for that. I suppose we could say we've been branded by that paw print of hers.